HELL OF A HELLO

The big redheaded man rubbed his knuckles, then reached for his drink on the bar.

The saloon was quiet, then someone said, "By damn, never seen Loonin bested before."

Loonin sat up and looked around until he found the man who had hit him. Slowly Loonin stood. He never took his cold stare off the redhead.

"Who the hell are you?" Loonin asked.

"Who the hell is asking?"

"My name is Rush Loonin. Always like to know the name of the gent I'm about to kill."

The redhead spoke. "My name is Canyon O'Grady—and did it ever occur to you that the dead one might be the likes of you?"

CANYON O'GRADY

6

COMSTOCK CRAZY

by

Jon Sharpe

A SIGNET BOOK

NEW AMERICAN LIBRARY

PUBLISHED BY
PENGUIN BOOKS CANADA LIMITED

PUBLISHER'S NOTE

This book is a work of fiction. Names, characters, places, and incidents either are the product of the author's imagination or are used fictitiously, and any resemblance to actual persons, living or dead, events, or locales is entirely coincidental.

The first chapter of this book appeared in
The Lincoln Assignment, the fifth volume in this series.

First Printing, March, 1990

2   3   4   5   6   7   8   9

Canyon O'Grady

His was a heritage of blackguards and poets, fighters and lovers, men who could draw a pistol and bed a lass with the same ease.

Freedom was a cry seared into Canyon O'Grady, justice a banner of the heart.

With the great wave of those who fled to America, the new land of hope and heartbreak, solace and savagery, he came to ride the untamed wildness of the Old West.

With a smile or a six-gun, Canyon O'Grady became a name feared by some and welcomed by others but remembered by all . . .

*1860, Virginia City, Utah Territory . . .
a town born out of "blue mud" and
the lure of fast wealth,
which now offered only the promise
of hard work and sudden death.*

1

Sweat beaded the medium-size man's forehead, and his eyes shot a quick glance at the door. It was too far away, and he knew he couldn't try, not and hold his head up again in this town.

Adolph Gathers swallowed, his prominent Adam's apple bobbing. Someone at a close by table laughed a skitterish, nervous, glad-I'm-not-you kind of sound.

"Look, Loonin, I didn't—"

"That's Mister Loonin to you, Gathers. Say it."

"Mr. Loonin, I did not mean to offend you. I had no idea you were standing behind me and—"

The man called Loonin was well over six feet tall and heavily built, his shoulders stretching the blue checkered shirt he wore. Now his fist snaked out and slammed into Gathers' cheek, jolting him along the bar as he scrabbled away, trying to maintain his feet.

Loonin went after Gathers like a bare-knuckled boxer, smashing his fists into the man as he hung on the bar until one, a solid right fist to the point of Gathers' jaw, sent him spinning to the floor. He hit a spittoon and it tipped over on his chest, the sour, fetid, brown juices splashing over him and soaking into his gray suit.

Gathers shook his head. For a few seconds he didn't seem to know where he was, then he pushed the spittoon away and started to stand up.

Loonin kicked Adolph in the stomach when he was on his hands and knees, flipping him on his back. The big man laughed and looked down at Gathers.

"You learn to keep your goddamn mouth shut, Gathers, or next time I'll knock all your teeth down your throat." Loonin pulled his right foot back to kick the downed man again. When he started it toward Gathers, someone behind Loonin slammed the big man's foot to the inside and it hit his own left leg. Loonin went down in a tangle of arms and legs, bellowing in pain.

Gathers scrambled up and ran out the front door.

Loonin came to his feet bellowing in rage. "Who's the bastard who hit me?" he roared. "I want to see the son of a bitch before I tear his head off."

A tall man near the bar took one more drink from a mug of beer and put it back on the varnished surface. With deliberate and calculated slowness he turned and stared at Loonin.

"I must be the son of a bitch you're looking for. I never liked to see a big lummox taking advantage of a smaller man." The speaker was four inches over six feet, heavily muscled at 220 pounds, and his hair was flame red. He had crackling blue eyes set in a roguish face.

Loonin roared and hurtled the ten feet across the room at his new target. But the redhead wasn't there when Loonin arrived. The bully met only a sharp, stinging left jab to his nose and then, as he slammed past and hit the bar, a heavy fist powered down into the unprotected back of Loonin's neck. His head snapped back and he almost passed out.

Loonin clutched at the bar much as Gathers had done before. The redhead stood four feet away watching him, his big hands at his sides; a fine leather holster was tied low on his thigh with a piece of rawhide.

"Stand still, you bastard," Loonin brayed as he pushed himself erect. His fists came up in the classic pose as he moved forward.

The redhead peppered his face with three hard jabs, bringing a spurt of blood from Loonin's nose before Loonin could even swing.

Again when Loonin lunged forward to hit the redhead, his opponent stepped away and this time tripped Loonin, sprawling him across a poker table while the four players hastily dived away for safety.

Loonin came up with a chair in his hands and swung it as he advanced on his tormentor.

As the chair passed him, the redhead darted back, then forward, caught the chair leg at the end of the swing, and jerked it forward. Loonin saw his mistake too late. He had hung on to the chair and already was moving toward the redhead. Three more hard blows thundered into Loonin. The final one was a smashing right to the side of his head that traveled no more than a foot.

Loonin's eyes closed, his knees buckled, and he fell backward to the floor, unconscious.

For a moment the saloon was quiet, then someone laughed.

"By damn, never seen Loonin bested before by anybody," a voice said.

"I want to buy that man a drink," another voice said.

The redhead stood, arms at his sides, watching Loonin as he shook his head trying to clear it. He sat up and looked around, then found the man who had hit him. Slowly Loonin stood. He never took his cold stare off the redhead.

"Who the hell are you?" Loonin asked.

"Who the hell is asking?"

"My name is Rush Loonin. Always like to know the name of the gent I'm about to kill."

All talk in the saloon died. Men who had been standing behind the two now separated so there was an open space behind each one in case a bullet missed its target.

They stood facing each other fifteen feet apart, their hands hanging loosely at their sides.

"The name is O'Grady. Did it ever occur to you that the dead one might be the likes of you?"

"No!"

Loonin began his draw first . . .

The men gasped as O'Grady ripped the Colt out of leather and fired so quickly that Loonin was still bringing his revolver up to aim. The slug from the .45 hit Loonin's wrist on the side, three inches above his thumb, jolted the weapon from his hand, and broke both his arm bones. He plowed backward into two chairs, dumped them over, and sat down hard, his left hand already holding his wounded wrist.

"Somebody get the doctor," Loonin bellowed.

"You can walk. Go over to his office yourself," O'Grady answered. Then he walked out of the saloon without a backward glance.

O'Grady wanted to find the small man called Gathers. He didn't have to look far. The man came out from the afternoon shadows of the Hansen General Store and fell into step beside O'Grady.

"I saw it all," Gathers said. "Nobody ever beat Loonin before, with his fists or with his gun. Damn! You did both. Mr. Moudry is gonna be terribly upset about this."

O'Grady turned, grinned at the smaller man, and held out his hand. "O'Grady is the name, you must be Gathers. Is there somewhere we can talk?"

"Absolutely. My store, Gathers' Mining Supply,

right down the block. I want . . ." He stopped. "Mr. O'Grady, I want to thank you for what you . . . for back there. I think he would have kicked me to death. He backed into me and spilled his beer on purpose just so he could beat me up."

"Why?"

They were at the front door of a twenty-foot-wide wooden building sandwiched in between two larger stores. Outside on the boardwalk were a collection of shovels, picks, star drills, sledges, and wheelbarrows.

Inside, a clerk nodded as they walked through to the back. Gathers had slipped out of his suit coat and vest, folding over the heavy brown stains and carrying the garments on his arm.

They went through a door and past a storeroom and to a smaller area to the side that had been partly walled off as an office. They sat in the only two chairs there.

Gathers had one eye swelling shut. His nose had bled, but now it had stopped and he carried his left arm as if it hurt.

"Do you want a drink, Mr. O'Grady? I'm afraid I need one." He took a whiskey bottle from a drawer in the small desk and found two glasses. He poured two fingers in each and sipped at his.

"Do you need to see the doctor?" O'Grady asked.

"No. I hurt, but I'll get over it. Nothing busted, thanks to you."

The man sipped the whiskey again and soon it was gone. He stared at the bottle, then pushed the cork in it and put it in his drawer.

"Now, Mr. Gathers, tell me what this is all about. I'm new in town and there's a lot I need to know."

"Simple. Loonin is a head-smasher for Edwin A. Moudry, owner of the Bonanza Mine, which is said to be the richest on Mount Davidson. He has half-dozen men who do exactly what Moudry tells them to do.

13

My son died in his mine three months ago, and I keep writing small articles about it in the newspaper, the *Territorial Enterprise*. I sign it with a pen name, but Moudry knows. This is his genteel way of telling me to stop."

"Does Moudry get his way around town, with the other mine-owners?"

"Usually. He has the biggest work force right now. He's even incorporating and selling stock in his mine in San Francisco. He cares nothing about the men who work for him."

Gathers sucked in a quick breath as a shiver of pain darted through him. He looked up. "Sorry. I don't handle pain well. Would you come home with me for some supper? Then we could talk and I'll tell you everything I know about Virginia City and Gold Hill."

"If it wouldn't be any trouble."

"Just me and my daughter at home now. My wife died ten years ago of the pox. Then Bill, three months ago. I still miss that boy. I wanted him to work in the store, but he said he could bring in more cash money in the mines. He did, until Moudry let him get killed."

After he talked to his clerk, Gathers came back, and he and Canyon walked out the back entrance.

Just as they closed the door in the alley, a rifle barked in the thin mountain air and a bullet whispered past and dug into the pine boards behind them.

2

Canyon O'Grady and Gathers both dived to the small dock and behind some heavy wooden boxes before a second shot blasted into the store's rear door. Two more shots sounded in the late-afternoon air as the men lay safe behind the boxes.

"Who in hell?" Gathers asked.

"Has to be my new friend, Rush Loonin, and his best rifle. A good thing he isn't a better shot. He was gunning at me, I'd say. Nice little town you've got here."

They waited five minutes, and when no more shots came, they darted into the back door of the store and left by the front.

"Anything you can tell me about this town I'd be right happy to hear," O'Grady said. "If your invitation is still open."

"Now more than ever. I owe you twice. Figure I'd be busted up and really bad off over at Doc Paulson's right now if you hadn't come along."

They walked two blocks, one straight up the hill from C Street, where the saloons, stores, hotels, and other commercial establishments had quickly sprung up.

The streets above that were terraced into the mountainside. Not a thought had been given to cross traffic up and down the slope. Moving from one street to another usually meant passing through someone's front yard, the next man's backyard, and then getting to B Street from C.

On B Street most of the more prosperous merchants had built their houses. These came in all sizes and shapes even a year after the great silver discovery. A few of the mine-owners had built large houses higher on what was called A Street, from where they could look out on their mine property and all the little people down the slopes.

Gathers quickly pointed this out to O'Grady as they took their walk.

"Down below C Street is D, where the poopsie girls live all in a ragged row. D Street has our famous whorehouses. There are more of them each month. Below them is China Town. Scattered around below them are the tents and the clapboard houses where hundred of miners live."

They snaked their way past a large house, along what had become a regular walkway, and came out on B Street. Three houses down, Gathers went up to a house and waved at it in pride.

"Not the biggest house on the street, but we're comfortable here," he said, opening the door.

The structure was two stories of wood construction with eight or ten rooms, O'Grady figured. As he looked around the well-furnished entrance hall and living room, a young woman came from a doorway and stood watching them, a smile on her pretty face.

"Father, I'm glad you're home," she said. She was slender, wore a print dress, and now carried a small towel in her hands. Her hair was softly flowing over her shoulders in a golden stream. Gentle blue eyes watched them. Her face was small, her mouth showing a curious smile as she watched the stranger.

O'Grady smiled at her. She had an interesting presence that he couldn't quite define. Not sexual, not motherly, more like a favorite aunt who was older and smarter but still half a child.

Gathers turned and nodded. "Ah, yes, my daughter, Nita. Sweetheart, I'd like to meet Mr. Canyon O'Grady. He's a special new friend and I want you to feed him a good supper." Gathers turned. "Mr. O'Grady, my daughter, Nita Gathers."

She smiled at him. "Pleased to meet you, Mr. O'Grady. Maybe you can explain why my father's looks like he's been in a roughhouse brawl."

"A slight difference of opinion is all, Miss Gathers," O'Grady said, holding his low-crowned brown hat with the wide brim.

"Not so slight," Gathers said. "Rush Loonin used me for a punching bag and a football until Mr. O'Grady here stepped in and sat the brute down on his pants. A fine sight it was."

The girl's expression turned cross and her words pleading. "Oh, Father. This is about those articles you're writing for Joe Goodman in the *Territorial Enterprise,* isn't it? I don't think they do any good and they certainly have gotten you in trouble again."

"Man's got a right to say what he wants to say. Joe agrees with me. Freedom of the press and all that."

"Lucky he hasn't had his print shop burned down yet," Nita said. She sighed. "I know I can't change you, Father, and I really don't want to. But I'm not wanting to go to another funeral again, either."

She watched the two of them. "We argue about this from time to time," she said to O'Grady in way of explanation. "Father, come into the kitchen and let me tend to that eye and your scrapes."

O'Grady went with them and found a large, friendly room with a new cooking range on one side, a big workbench along one wall, and a six-foot plank kitchen table set for two. Nita worked quickly over her father's eye, putting on a poultice of some kind. She said it would help reduce the swelling and the discoloration.

"You hold that over your eye until time for supper. Then maybe you'll be able to see what you're eating." She looked at O'Grady. "I hope you're not expecting a banquet. You'll have to make do with what I'm cooking."

"I'm sure whatever you have will be fine," O'Grady said.

She shooed them both out of the kitchen and they settled down in the comfortable living room with its fireplace.

Gathers looked up with his one good eye. "You had some questions about the town?" he asked.

"Yes, a lot. As I understand it, the placer workings are all done and now it's a matter of digging down to find the mother lode, the veins of silver in the hard rock."

"Yes, the first men here have mostly left to hunt for gold they can pan. They didn't like the idea of digging deep into the mountain, and that's where the silver is. A hard-rock man has got to be willing to go wherever the vein of silver leads him."

"How deep are they now? In my first quick look I didn't see any big machinery operating."

"No, not yet. That will come in a few years. Right now two of the mines are down a little over a hundred feet, bringing up the ore and worthless rock by windlass, man-powered. That can't last much longer."

"And you think they'll go deeper?" O'Grady asked.

"Deeper? Oh, yes, three hundred, four hundred feet, maybe as much as fifteen hundred feet or a mile down. Depends where the vein goes."

"What happens if you and I have claims adjacent to

each other, you dig down and hit a vein, and it runs directly into my claim far underground?''

"According to the law here, the man who finds the vein owns it, wherever it goes. As we dig more lateral tunnels, that might change, who can tell?''

"Who is this man, Edwin Moudry, you've been talking about?''

"Biggest mine-owner on the hill. He also has the most money to develop it. The old saying is that you've got to own a gold mine in order to work a silver mine. Silver mining is expensive, the silver isn't just lying there like gold is. A lot harder to get the pure silver out of the ore.''

"From what I've heard, Moudry isn't exactly a Sunday-school teacher.''

"He'd send his blind grandmother down into the gopher hole if he thought she could dig out ore for him,'' Gathers said.

"He's got more than one bully boy like Rush Loonin, then?'' O'Grady asked.

"Indeed he does. He keeps five or six. There are fifteen or twenty gunslingers around town who can be bought by anyone with the required wages.''

"Not much law in town?'' O'Grady asked.

"Not much. One U.S. marshal who is overworked and getting tired. Then there's a territorial judge appointed by President Buchanan. He's usually over at Genoa, and he can be bought by the side that offers the most gold.''

"Sounds about like the quality of other territorial governments and judges I've met so far, I'd guess. This marshal, is he any good?''

"Straight and true, but overworked. Think how it's going to be in Virginia City when we have ten thousand people here and just one U.S. marshal for law.

Maybe by then we'll have a city marshal and some deputies or a police force.''

''That I'd hope would happen, eventually. You ever hear of a surveyor and mine inspector named Luke Denker?'' Canyon asked.

''Denker, Denker. Can't be sure of the name, but that sounds like the handle of the agent who got killed a couple of months ago. Heard he was some kind of government man. That would be the mine-inspector part, I'd guess.''

''What happened?''

''Story about it in the *Enterprise*. Don't recall exactly, but seems like it was a small cave-in while he was inspecting the Bonanza. Know it happened at the Bonanza.''

''Interesting. Friend of his asked me to look into it if I was in this area. You said your son was killed in the Bonanza as well?''

''Yes. They were just starting to dig out laterally in tunnels from the shafts and then sending the shafts down deeper. The rope broke on the windlass one day just as three miners started down in a bucket. They fell over a hundred feet. Two weeks after that they started using twisted-steel cable on the windlass. If they'd started using it two weeks earlier—just two damn weeks!—then Billy would still be alive.''

''How many major mines are there operating now?''

''Here on Mount Davidson there are five. Those are the outfits that got financing and bought up a lot of the surface claims the placer men owned. Strange what some men will sell out for when the gold isn't right there waiting for his pan. Men are still selling thirty- and fifty-foot chunks of their claims. I know some of them are selling out a fortune, but no way I can convince them.''

"How many people you think are in town now, Mr. Gathers?"

"Hard to tell. A thousand, maybe five times that out in the gullies and on the mountain. Don't think anybody ever counted."

Nita came in. She had brushed her hair until it shone and added a touch of raspberry juice to her red lips. She smiled at Canyon.

"Our dinner is ready," she said, then stepped aside and let the man walk into the kitchen first.

They had mashed potatoes and brown bacon gravy, long-cooked carrots, and a roasted chicken. The bread, fresh from the oven, hadn't quite cooled down yet, and there were butter and strawberry preserves. For dessert there was apple pie and fresh whipped cream.

Canyon O'Grady leaned back and grinned at Nita. "I'm glad you didn't put on a feast. I don't know what I'd have done. I don't get a lot of home cooking, so I appreciate this meal tonight. It was outstanding."

She ducked her head, mumbled a thank you, and soon stood and excused herself.

"What brings you to town, Mr. O'Grady," Gathers asked.

O'Grady shrugged. "Hard to tell for sure. I might want to invest in some mining property myself. Then again I might just settle down and start a little store. I'd say this is going to be a longtime community here at Virginia City. Place a man can put down some roots and develop a life for himself."

"I figured that way about eight months ago," Gathers said. "Never been sorry. If it wasn't for Moudry and his bully boys, this would be a fine little community."

"One of these days someone might upset Mr. Moudry's plans. Well, I thank you again for your fine supper and the background on the town. Now I better be getting back to the hotel." They shook hands and O'Grady hurried back down to C Street and found the door marked U.S. MARSHAL'S OFFICE.

He went in and saw a tall slender man sitting behind a desk. He was not over thirty, with a lean face, eyes the color of the Mississippi river at flood tide, and a grin that lit up the room.

"Marshal?"

The man stood. "Right, Marshal Ben Jones. I'd bet half a month's pay that you're this Canyon O'Grady I've been hearing about."

"Guilty, Marshal Jones. We need to talk." O'Grady reached in his pocket and took out a purse. From inside a small compartment he extracted a sturdy printed card with a tintype photo glued to it. He handed it to the marshal, who looked at it.

He read the statement that the bearer, Canyon O'Grady, was a United States agent charged with enforcing the laws of the United States and territories. The card asked all law-enforcement agencies to cooperate with the agent in every way possible. The card carried a picture of O'Grady and was signed by President Buchanan.

"Well, well. I'd heard there were such men around, but I've never bumped into one of you before. Sit down. Welcome to Virginia City. What brings you to town and how can I help?"

"Briefly I'm here concerning Luke Denker, Marshal. I want to find out how he died and if it was really an accident, and if not, then who killed him. Denker was a U.S. government employee."

"Be glad to give you what I have. The Bonanza people cooperated, showed me the tunnel where he died. A square set just gave way and about a ton of rock and dirt hit him. I was there when they dug him out. It was at the hundred-foot level. Only the second time I've been down that far. I don't like it underground.''

"You make a written report? I've never seen anything on it.''

"Yep, but the report stayed here. I didn't know who to send it to. You're more than welcome to look at it. Just as a warning, while you're in town, I'd suggest you watch your back. Rush Loonin ain't a man to take lightly what you did to him in that saloon.''

"I've heard. Somebody already took a shot at me. Seems you don't have a friendly town here.''

"We try. I need some help, but they won't authorize me to hire any deputies.'' Jones pushed a handwritten sheet across his desk to O'Grady. "Take a look. Don't think it'll help much. Denker was inspecting the Bonanza at the time. Evidently nobody saw the cave-in.''

O'Grady read through the report. It didn't help. He handed it back. "Any feeling on Denker? Was he liked in town? Did his job put him at odds with the mineowners? Did he have any real enemies?''

Jones put a western wide-brimmed hat on and settled it in place, then he leaned back in his chair and looked at the ceiling.

"Yeah, his job put him against the mine-owners more often than not. He told them things they had to fix and what they could do with the miners. Never been much control by the federal government before on mines. The owners didn't like it. But one of them going as far as to kill him . . . I wouldn't think so.

" 'Far as I could tell the men liked him. He was welcome in the saloons and the poker games. Friendly guy, bachelor. Told me once he figured he'd be here for maybe ten years the way the silver was showing up underground.''

"He say anything about any threats? Maybe some of Moudry's bully boys pushed him around.''

"Nope, not a hint of that from him, or from around town."

O'Grady stood. "Well, it figured not to be easy. I'll have to do some digging myself. Anything you can help me with will be appreciated. Oh, I'm sub-rosa on this one. Appreciate your not telling anyone I work for your boss."

"Easy and done. Remember to watch for Loonin. I know he's killed two men here, but I don't have enough evidence to prove it."

"I always watch my back." They shook hands and O'Grady went into the street. It was starting to merge toward dusk. O'Grady turned toward his hotel and saw a man in front of him. He had been leaning against the wall but now came alert, moved onto the boardwalk, blocking O'Grady's path. The stranger moved his right hand and a long-bladed knife glinted in the lamplight from the saloon next door.

A small sound behind him made O'Grady turn his head. A second man ten feet behind him had pushed away from the wall and moved toward the agent, a knife in each hand and a vicious sneer on his face.

3

O'Grady met the closest man with a blast from his .45 Colt. The slug hit the man in the right shoulder, spinning him around and jolting the knife from his hand. O'Grady turned in an instant, but he was almost too late. The man behind him had charged, knife at arm's length like a lance.

There was no time to shoot. O'Grady swept his heavy six-gun in front of him, hitting the right hand that held the knife and thrusting it aside. He dropped backward on the boardwalk, pulled the second knife-man with him, and pushed his feet in the man's chest. As he fell, O'Grady threw the slicer over his head down the boardwalk. The second attacker landed on his back and shoulders with a crunch.

In the maneuver O'Grady had dropped his six-gun. He looked for it in the gathering darkness, but the first attacker was back, the long knife now in his left hand. He seemed to use it as well there as in his right.

O'Grady's knife was in his right boot. He swept it out as he sprang to his feet. His five-inch blade was broad and heavy, a fighting knife sharpened on both sides of the tip to slice either way.

He swung the blade in front of him as the wounded man came forward. A feint to the left and to the right didn't deter the attacker. He held the six-inch blade as a knife-fighter who knew what he was doing: his hand wrapped around the handle with the blade pointing directly forward. It allowed the user to stab ahead or slice in either directions without changing the grip.

The two men feinted one way, then the other, neither wanting to make the first move.

O'Grady growled deep in his throat, trying to show the man his impatience. He feinted one way, back the other, then jolted forward a step as if lunging. He stopped suddenly and in a split second the other man powered forward, unable to stop his countermove. He surged across where O'Grady would have been with his blade committed.

O'Grady drove forward at the last moment when the man was off balance, thrust the heavy blade through the man's right biceps, and slashed it out. This one wouldn't be knife-fighting for a while.

The man roared in pain, fell to the boardwalk, rolled to his feet like an acrobat, and ran away down the dusty street.

When O'Grady looked back at the man he had thrown over his head, he found him on both knees, a derringer in his hand. The gunman was twelve feet away, a long shot for a derringer for any kind of accuracy.

O'Grady's boot touched his own iron. He swept down, grabbed it, and came upright just as the other man fired. O'Grady's answering shot came almost on top of the first one. The derringer lead whizzed past O'Grady, missing his side by inches. The agent's round smashed into the gunman's chest, shattering his sternum and slanting slightly downward. Half the .45 slug tore into the left side of the attacker's heart.

The gunman's eyes went wide in the pale light, one hand came up to his chest. He looked in surprise at O'Grady, then a last ragged rush of air came from his lungs and he fell forward, his face scraping against the rough boards in front of the general store.

"What the hell?" Marshal Ben Jones growled as he rushed out of his office door. He looked at O'Grady. "One tried for you right on my doorstep?"

"No, two of them. You'll find the second one at your doctor's office, I'd guess. He's got a slug in his right arm and a big cut on his left arm. My guess is that both of these men are drifters who were hired by our friend Mr. Loonin. The hard part is, unless one of them talks, this will all be hard to prove."

"Let's go see the doctor."

They left the body where it had fallen and walked down the street a full block to where Dr. Paulson had his office with his quarters behind it. There was a light on and the office door was half-open.

A bell rang as they went into the office, triggered by the movement of the door top.

"Be right out," a voice called from a back room.

Marshal Jones motioned forward and the two men walked through rooms toward the voice. Two doors down they saw a light. Inside the room a man sat in a chair while a small, potbellied man with red cheeks put a bandage on the patient's left arm.

"Don't do too good a job, Doc Paulson, that man's under arrest and is sure to hang."

"See here . . ." the medic began, then he saw it was the marshal. The doctor moved to the man's right arm and cut away the upper part of the shirt sleeve.

"He said it was a friendly little card game."

"Not all that friendly, looks like," O'Grady said. "What I want to know is who hired you to kill me." He grabbed the wounded man's jaw in his big hand.

"Nobody. I was in a card game."

"Sure you were, and you've got twenty witnesses to

prove it. You waited for me to come out of the marshal's office and then you and your dead friend tried to kill me. Who hired you?''

The man looked around, his eyes wide now, fear tingeing the expression on his face through three days' growth of beard. "He didn't say kill you, said just cut you up some, make you go away.''

"That's better," O'Grady said. "What's his name?''

"He'll kill me sure.''

"You're going to hang anyway," Marshal Jones said. "You were in a criminal attack where a man died. Don't matter who it was or if you pulled the trigger or not. That's murder and you'll hang. Why not take this guy who hired you to the gallows with you? What do you owe him?''

The hired gun looked at the lawman. His face worked and he lifted his left hand painfully and rubbed his nose. "If I tell you, then he could hang, too?''

"Damn right. He started it all.''

"Hell, why not? Bastard wouldn't protect me. I done some other things for him.''

"What's his name?''

"Hell, you know him already. His name is—''

A booming shot thundered into the closed room, deafening the three men inside. O'Grady knew at once what had happened. He recovered first and dived toward the door. He heard footsteps: before he got out the door and through the hall, the gunman had rushed into the darkness of the street.

O'Grady took one shot at the vanishing form in the night, but didn't think he made contact. The man was gone. Back inside the doctor's treatment room, he knew what he would find.

Dr. Paulson had just folded the man's hands in front of him. There was a small hole through the patient's blue shirt and a gout of blood on the wall behind him.

28

O'Grady stared at the closed eyes.

"I'm afraid your witness is dead," Dr. Paulson said.

"One more point for Rush Loonin and Edwin Moudry," O'Grady said. "But his winning hand is about to turn sour on him."

The marshal and O'Grady walked out of the office and stood on the street.

"Who knows the most about everyone in town?" O'Grady asked the lawman.

"Well, usually that would be the Catholic priest, but we don't have one here yet. Next it would probably be the local sheriff, but we aren't a county seat so we don't have one of those either. Outside of that, I'd have to say it's the most popular madam in town. That would be Julia Cosette. She's run out three other houses and has all the business to herself, at least right now."

"Sounds like she's a lady I should go see."

"Just don't call her a lady. She's a bit sensitive about that. Says her mother was a lady; she's a woman and damn proud of it."

O'Grady took the directions and walked down to D Street and found the best house on the block. It was a large wood frame building that had been brick-faced on one side and the front. He went up the well-painted steps to a varnished solid-oak door and saw a small sign that said, OPEN—PLEASE COME IN.

He did.

The reception area was twenty feet square. A man in red suspenders over a white shirt and a derby hat, played piano at an upright with its front removed. He was banging out "The Girl I Left Behind."

A woman came from behind a beaded-curtain doorway and smiled at O'Grady. She wore an evening gown much like he had seen at some of the fancy Washington balls. No more breast showed here than had in Washington, D.C., and that amounted to about half of each marvelous orb. She had a tight little waist and walked toward him, letting everything that wanted to bounce and sway.

"Good evening, sir. How may we be of service to you tonight?" The girl said it with a refined New England twang to her voice. Her smile seemed genuine.

"I'm here to see Miss Cosette on some personal business. Is she busy?"

"Oh. Too bad." For just a moment her mask slipped and she grinned. "Christ, I ain't seen a hunk of man like you in three months." She said it softly so no one else could hear. Then the mask slid back in place.

"I'll go see if Miss Cosette can talk to you. Do you have a name or a business card?"

"Canyon O'Grady."

Her eyes lit up at once. Her grin came back through the mask. "Oh, damn! You're the one who put Rush Loonin on his can and shot his gun wrist. Julia will bust a tit to see you." The girl recovered. "I'm sorry for the outburst. Would you please come this way?"

News traveled fast in Virginia City.

They walked through the parlor into a short hallway and down two doors. The girl knocked, then opened the door a crack and whispered something through the opening.

The door swung wide and Canyon O'Grady had his first look at Julia Cosette. She stood about five-two and had the largest breasts he'd ever seen on a slender woman. Her age could have been twenty-five to forty. Her skin was clear, without a blemish, and soft and creamy white.

She wore a short evening gown that covered her only to her knees, and came around her neck, but was cinched up at the waist with a wide belt. Piles of red hair billowed down from her head, spreading across her shoulders, dipping below her waist in front and more raining down her back.

Her liquid green eyes stared at him just a moment and then her face disintegrated in a roaring laugh.

"I'll be damned. You had to be a redhead. I just knew it. Come in and relax a minute and let me look at you. I know men, and there hasn't been one like you through here since we opened up this jackass mining operation."

The welcome girl had faded out the door. When Canyon took his glance off the woman, he saw that her room matched her style. It was a whore's room; garish satin drapes covered one whole wall, and the wallpaper on the other walls was full of cupids, arrows, and lovers. The furniture was overstuffed, expensive. A canopied bed stood in the far corner, a masterpiece of wood carving and ornamentation, the bedding all frills and satins and half a dozen highly colored matched pillows. He was sure the sheets were made of silk.

"So . . ." she said, walking around him. "What's on your mind?"

"Miss Cosette, a friend of mine came to town and is buried here. I'm trying to find out what happened. Seems he met his death under a ton of rock in the Bonanza about a hundred feet underground while on a regular inspection trip."

The woman sat down in one of the soft chairs and pointed to one nearby.

"That would be Luke Denker, a gent about thirty-five who was a surveyor and a government mine inspector. Your source was right, I know most of the men in town. Still can for a while. But the way them galoots are finding silver, that won't last long. Soon we're gonna have ten thousand people in here."

"Did Luke die under a cave-in or was that just a cover-up for how he really died?"

Julia rolled a cigarette in a paper, licked the seal, and finished it, then lit it with a match she struck on the underside of the chair's arm. When she blew away the smoke, she nodded. "Oh, he died in the mine, for damn sure. But I don't know why or how. The cave-in was a farce. No well-placed square set ever gave way on the edge of a tunnel like that. But with no witnesses, how can you hang anybody for murder?"

"Is that your professional opinion?"

"Whose profession, yours or mine?"

"Both."

"Oh, not much doubt about it. Half the people who stop and think figure that Moudry had the man killed. The big problem is that knowing it and proving it are two different kettles of fish. Way I look at it is, don't matter much why a snake gets killed, as long as it gets done all legal and proper. One murder conviction is about as good as another one."

Canyon O'Grady grinned. "You're quite a philosopher, Miss Cosette."

"Call me Julia. Hey, I'll make a small bet with you. Are you game?"

"Why not, Julia, why not?"

"I bet that you've never paid a woman to make love to you, am I right?"

"Right. Don't you ever make a mistake?"

"I did once when I was fourteen. My uncle said he just wanted to see if the bedbugs had bitten me so he could put medicine on the bites. I let him take my clothes off so he could be sure. He was sure, all right. My dad caught us on the fifth go-round. He shot my uncle dead and booted me out of the house."

She watched him, then stood and held out her hand. "I was right. I won the bet, now you pay off."

He stood, a slight frown staining his features. "So?"

She tugged a minute at a fastener at the front of her dress and a moment later the whole bodice slid down to show her big breasts.

"So you lost the bet. You have to pleasure me on my featherbed." She pulled him toward the bed at the side of the room.

"And if I'd won the bet?" Canyon asked.

"Oh, then I would have had to pleasure you. Kind of I win, you lose."

O'Grady shook his head. "Not a chance of me losing. This way I'd say that we both get to win."

She laughed softly, reached up, and kissed him, then they both fell gently onto the soft bed.

4

Julia kissed O'Grady deliciously, like he was a favorite piece of candy she couldn't eat fast enough. Then she pushed back a little so her eyes could focus on his face.

"Make you another bet, glorious man. I'd say you're a guy who likes to undress his women."

"You win again, but then it's your house." O'Grady leaned in and kissed one of her breasts. She murmured deep in her throat and he kissed the orb again, then licked her nipple.

"Gawd! No man's done that for me in five years!" She lifted his chin, pushing his face away from her breast so she could see him. "You want to move in and get serviced twice a day for the rest of your life?"

"At that rate I'd live about a month and die smiling. Sit up, so I can appreciate what I see."

Julia laughed and sat up on the bed, pulling her dress top down more. When she sat, her breasts swung out like twin mountains on their sides, with a heavy crease of cleavage between them. Her wide areolae were bright pink and her nipples a deeper shade.

He kissed from one to the other nipple down through the valley and up the other side, then he pulled one breast into his mouth and chewed until she yelped in delight.

She turned so he could unfasten the back of her

dress, then she moved enough so she could lift it over her head. She kicked out of three petticoats and then sat there on the soft bed wearing only some filmy, silk short panties.

Then she undressed him slowly. "You're really going to go after Moudry, aren't you, O'Grady?"

"If he's the man who had Denker killed, I am. First I need to establish that to my best satisfaction."

"Satisfaction is what I guarantee here. I don't want you to horn in on my trade." She giggled at her little joke.

A minute later she had stripped off his boots and clothes and he stretched out beside her.

"How did you happen to land here, Julia?"

"I got escorted out of Salt Lake City by a local committee. They didn't like my working in the hotel there. I was heading for San Francisco when I heard about the strike over here. I was in Carson City resting up after a long stage ride and I found two girls. We decided to come up here and work awhile. It's worked out rather well and looks good for ten years."

"Business is that good?"

"Great. There are three of man's favorite activities that it's hard to fail at if you provide those services: fucking, gambling, and drinking. I provide my facilities here as a kind of public service to the community. So far the town has responded well. 'Course, there ain't a lot of married men here yet, with their wives and kids. That's gonna cause some problems, always does."

They both laughed softly and he caught her breasts and caressed them like precious jewels. Then he kissed her and slowly brought one hand up her leg.

"Oh, God," Julia panted. "Oh, God."

O'Grady moved his other hand down to her legs and rubbed them gently, moving higher and higher. Her breathing began to speed up and soon she was moaning.

"Oh, Lordy, but you have the touch, O'Grady. Oh, damn!"

He stroked her button a half-dozen times and Julia began to croon. Soon she shivered and shook and gasped through a strong climax. He kept stroking her button and she paused a moment, then surged into a series of vibrations that set her moaning loud and long until the pleasures rolled away and she mewed and snuggled against him.

"Oh, Lordy, I done died and gone to heaven." She looked up at him. "You have any idea how often a whore gets treated to her own pleasures, let alone gets done first? About one out of a thousand, if she's lucky. Oh, God, I never want it to change, never want to leave this spot, not in a hundred years."

They lay there until she was breathing normally again. Then suddenly she rolled toward him and dropped one of her breasts into his mouth. Her hands moved down his belly to his erection, teased it, and then caught it and stroke it.

"Oh, my, yes, you are ready." She bent and kissed the purple head, then came back and lay fully on top of him. "This way you won't have to do any of the work."

She moved lower, angled his lance upward, and expertly slid down on him until they were connected pelvic bone to pelvic bone. Gently she began to move, to tighten her inside muscles, squeezing him with each change in direction.

Gradually she increased the motion until she was working forward and back and at the same time up and down. It was as if she were riding a pony.

"Oh, my, yes," Julia whispered. She went faster and faster.

O'Grady had submitted to her wishes and now, almost before he knew it, he was panting and his hips began to grind and thrust upward to meet her downward strokes.

She increased the motion more and the squeezings came faster and then his breath gushed in gasps as he bellowed out a roar that he was sure they could hear in the deepest coyote hole on the mountain. But he didn't care.

Seldom had he been manipulated so skillfully. Almost never had he been so worked up that he cried out just before his own climax. O'Grady gave another roar, then slammed his hips into the air, lifting the small lady higher still as he jolted six hard shots into her waiting vessel.

He collapsed onto the featherbed and Julia eased down on top of him, covering him, protecting him. She was panting herself from another climax. A smile wreathed her face as she lay there.

She eventually opened her eyes.

O'Grady was watching her. "Little lady, you are some kind of woman. You really got my old horse to galloping all the way home."

"It was a fine ride for me, too. Hope you're not in a hurry. I'll get us a bite of supper from the kitchen in a bit."

"Not in a hurry, but that pony ride you gave me sure did make me hungry."

"Good."

"You do a mighty fine bit of loving," Canyon said.

"Nice to hear." Julia was pleased.

5

Well up on the side of Mount Davidson overlooking the ragtag collection of houses and stores and the sea of tents that formed a growing Virginia City, a finely built mine office lifted toward the sky. It was already two stories high and a third one was in the process of construction. In the lower portion in his temporary office sat Edwin A. Moudry.

Moudry wore a fifty-dollar suit from San Francisco's best tailor. A gold nugget the size of a fifty-cent piece dangled from a gold chain from his vest watch pockets. The blue suit had the hint of a pinstripe, and his shirt had a ruffle at the throat and down the front—the latest in fashion in San Francisco.

He was a well-fed man who carried 180 pounds on his five-foot-six-inch frame. Heavy arms and shoulders betrayed his early days as a hard-rock miner. Now he lit a fifty-cent cigar—half a day's wages for most workers in Virginia City—and stared out the big window over the valley.

His face was broad and plain, no mustache or beard, only pouting lips, thin and colorless, a slightly bent nose from a difference of opinion in a saloon fight when he was much younger, and pale-gray eyes that looked as if they were leaking his bodily fluids. He touched a linen handkerchief to his eyes and blinked, then turned and stared at Rush Loonin.

"He shot your arm when he had your whole body to aim at?" Moudry shook his head. "Loonin, you should be dead right now, you know that, I trust."

"Yes, sir, Mr. Moudry. He's good and he's fast, but I've taken care of more dangerous men before for you. I and my friends can do it again."

"Your friends like the two you had to pay two dollars each for a burial? I can't afford that kind of publicity. It was just by chance you stopped that second man before he talked."

Moudry stood and walked to the window. There was a slight limp from a mine accident years ago. Now his forty-eight years showed as he moved.

After a long pull on the cigar and a leisurely expelling of the smoke, he stared down the barren, desert-dry canyon. "The problem now is what should we do next?"

He stared at Loonin. After a pause he nodded. "Thanks for the help, Rush. I should have known. What did you find out about this fast gun? Where is he from? What is he doing here? What does he want?"

"He talked to the marshal, but I ain't gonna ask the lawman what that was about. Last time I seen O'Grady he was going into Julia's house."

"Damn. Julia knows almost everything that goes on in this town. Keep looking. Talk to your saloon friends. Get one of your men to questions the whores. Somebody's got to know why he's here. Where's he staying?"

"Big Strike Hotel. He didn't sleep there last night. Must have slept over with the whores."

"At least we know he has one weakness. Get out of here and see what you can find out. If he talked with the marshal, he could be some kind of a lawman. So be damned careful. Don't try to kill him. Not before we even know why he's here. Forget that he beat you.

Don't worry about that. You worry about keeping your job with me.''

"Yes, sir, Mr. Moudry. I'll learn everything there is to know about him. That little whore Wanda will be a help." He turned his hat around and around in his hands. His right wrist and arm held a heavy plaster cast from wrist to elbow. When he moved the arm, pain showed on his face.

"That's all, Loonin. Next time you be more careful or I'll be spending two dollars on a coffin for you."

Loonin nodded and went out the door quickly into the hall.

Another door into the big office opened and a young woman came in. She went directly to Moudry and rubbed his temples from where she stood behind his big chair.

"Problems, sweet daddy?" she asked. She wore a robe and now let it part in front as she moved around and sat in his lap.

He pushed the robe open and fondled one of her breasts, kneading it gently, making her purr. "Nothing I can't take care of." His hands curled around her breast and lifted it. He bent and kissed it, then bit her nipple until she moaned in delight.

"Damn but I love this. Used to be I dreamed of getting me a woman whenever I wanted her, twice, three, four times a day." He tried to reach her crotch but couldn't the way they sat. "Damn nice what money can buy, Belle, don't you agree?"

"Dresses and gowns and jewels, money buys them. But you ain't bought me, Eddie. You're just renting me. I can pull out of here anytime I want to."

"But you won't. You like the money. And you don't get pawed and poked ten times a day by all of those dirty, smelly miners."

"True." She sighed. "But sometimes you don't

40

poke me enough. I need it more than most women. How about right now?'' She stood and slid the robe off her shoulders and let it fall to the floor. Her long black hair came nearly to her waist and she brushed it back from large breasts that jiggled and bounced as she moved her shoulders. She was plump, with a generous ass and heavy thighs. A pure black swatch of dark hair struggled to cover her crotch.

Moudry's hand reached out and spread her legs and probed and stroked her, then shook his head and gently eased her away from him as he pulled up to the desk. "Later. Right now I've got to figure out something that's gonna make us one hell of a lot of money.''

"Besides the mine? You said it was good for five million dollars in silver.''

"It is. The Bonanza will pay off, but it costs a lot to dig it out and then break up the ore and at last get the silver. I'm working another little plan that will multiply the value of that silver.''

Belle shrugged, bent, and picked up the robe. Her bottom came close to Moudry. He looked over and slapped her buttocks. Belle laughed, pulled on the robe, and went out the door she had come in.

Moudry looked at the figures he had written on a sheet of paper in front of him. He was getting about 20 percent gold out of his current diggings. The silver ore was harder to extract. Eventually there would be a way to do it right there in the Washoe River. Until then a lot of his top quality ore was being shipped out by mule train.

He pondered it. If the silver were processed right there, it would be easy. Moudry looked for a better way to get rich faster. If he couldn't steal gold or silver going out of the hill, what was there of value? He pondered it for several minutes, then he began to grin.

He checked the number of men working his mine.

There were almost five times that many on the hill, and six months ago the owners had got together and worked out a simple plan. Yes. It had been a good idea; it still was, and it was tailor-made for his operation.

The mine-owners' plan would be implemented in two weeks, and Moudry would be ready. He laughed softly and began estimating what he would make on such a move. He put several figures down, then nodded. That was about what he could expect.

The figure showed a take of about fifty-two thousand dollars, all in cash. That would mean a straight profit for him of over thirty-nine thousand. Not bad for an evening's work. It wasn't a million, but what the hell. Easy way to make a dollar.

That settled, he went back to his desk and stared out the window. Now, what the hell about this small problem, one Canyon O'Grady? Irish. He never had liked the Irish. Now he had a double reason. If that lout Loonin couldn't find out enough about O'Grady, he'd use Belle. She had an interesting way of working on a man to get him to tell her almost anything. Yes, Belle might come in handy that way.

Thinking of Belle, he wondered if she still had those black lacy frilly things. He'd just solved a problem and he had earned a reward. Belle would be the reward. He smiled as he stood, rubbed his crotch, and walked through the door into Belle's room. She sat on her big bed naked and had one hand on her crotch. Her face beamed as he came in.

"Hey, glad you got here. I had to start without you."

Three long blocks away, Canyon O'Grady eased out of bed, trying not to awaken the woman beside him. He slipped into his underwear and pants, then laced up his boots. When he looked back at the bed, Julia sat watching him, bare to the waist.

"We don't serve breakfast around here. Most of us sleep until noon. The Beanery is about the best breakfast in town. You tell Elly Handshoe I sent you there. She cooks a mean breakfast besides beans."

She stood on the bed so she was as tall as he was, walked across the feather mattress, and put her arms around him. She was taller than he was. Julia kissed him hard on the lips and eased back. "You come back, cowboy, you hear me? This can't be a one-night romp. I got to be with you more than this." She shrugged again. "Even just to talk. You're real people. Hell, I understand what you're saying, how you feel. You come back or I'll come find you."

He kissed her back and helped her to the floor.

"Yes, ma'am, I'll be back. Right now I got me some rows of potatoes to hoe."

He finished dressing and opened the door. He was about to say good-bye, but saw she was sleeping again. He closed the door, found his way out the back of the whorehouse, and went past the rear of a business and between buildings to C Street in the local manner.

He found the Beanery and settled in at a counter that only had one other empty stool. Behind him were six small tables with four men around each.

A woman stomped up to the counter and stared at O'Grady. "You want the full breakfast?" she snapped.

O'Grady figured she must by Elly, so he gave her his best smile. "That would be wonderful, and some coffee, if it's not too much trouble."

"No trouble at all. You that new fast gun in town?"

"Name is Canyon O'Grady."

"Yeah, figured." She looked at him a moment in an honest, open appraisal, then nodded. "I'm Elly Handshoe. Have your grub up in a minute." She went behind a partition and sooner than he expected was back with a pint coffeecup filled to the brim. When she came back a moment later it was with a large tin plate piled with food.

She put it in front of him, clattered down silverware, and pushed pots of jam and syrup and butter toward him. "Here's a start, you want more for thirty cents, you holler." Then Elly was gone.

Canyon looked at the plate of food. Highest was a stack of six big hotcakes with two fried eggs on top. Below that were three more eggs, fried sunny-side-up and spread over a carpet of fried potatoes and onions. Eight thick slices of bacon lay to one side.

Twenty minutes later he had just cleaned his plate when Elly stopped in front of him.

"Want another helping?" she asked.

"No, no. That was more than I needed. Delicious. Elly, when you have a minute I'd like to talk to you."

"Yeah? I ain't buying nothing if you're selling." She watched him closely.

"Nothing like that."

She watched him a few seconds, then nodded. "All right. I got about five minutes. Over there at that clean table."

They sat by the window as the breakfast trade slowed.

"Do you remember a man named Luke Denker?"

"Luke? Of course. Ate here all the time. Damned good man. Shame he got buried down in the Bonanza."

"You hear anything about it being a little unusual, strange?"

Elly Handshoe looked at him sharply. "Like somebody killed him and then dropped that square set out so he'd get a ton of rock on his skull? Sure. Heard it from the first day. But that was the Bonanza, who's going to check?''

"So you think there was foul play?"

Elly lifted her brows. "Who can say? But talk like this ain't exactly popular in this town, especially around the Bonanza folks. You staying at the hotel or you want a spot in my boardinghouse? I got the best of everything. Even do up your wash you need it.''

"Thanks, but I better stick to the hotel for a time. Just looking around town.''

Elly stood. "Well, enjoy. You want another good meal or a good bed, come back.'' She turned and walked behind the counter and began clearing dishes.

O'Grady left and headed for the Big Strike Hotel and his room and his gear. It was intact. He had just washed up in the porcelain bowl in the room and changed clothes when there was a knock at his door.

He drew his six-gun and cocked it as he walked to the door, then stood to the side, unlocked it, and cracked it open an inch. He saw a girl, Nita Gathers. "Yes?"

"Oh, Mr. O'Grady, I'm so glad I found you. There are two men down at the store and Father told me to come and find you. If you don't come and talk to them, they say they're going to kill him."

6

Canyon opened the door wide and drew Nita Gathers into his hotel room. Her face showed white with fear, eyes wild, her breath coming quickly. "Calm down, Nita. Tell me, what did those two men look like?"

"I know one of them. He's Loonin, a big man. He's the one who hurt Father before. He's mean. You've got to come right away!"

O'Grady holstered his Colt, grabbed his hat, and led the shivering girl out the door. As they walked, he found out what he wanted to know.

"Where is your father?"

"In the back room. They tied him up in a chair. He can't move at all."

"How close to the back door? Is it locked?"

"He's ten, fifteen feet away from the door. We went in that way this morning, so it was unlocked then. I can't say about now. I don't think it was locked when I left."

They walked partway toward the store, then stopped.

"Nita, I want you to go to the store. Wait outside and give me enough time to get around to the back door. Then you run in the front door screaming, saying that you couldn't find me and not to shoot your father. When you burst in, I'll have a chance to surprise them. You understand?"

Nita nodded, her long blond hair bobbing, but her soft blue eyes still were frightened.

"Give me two or three minutes to get around to the back door." Canyon took off at a trot to the narrow alley in back of the store and ran along it until he could see the rear door. He hurried up to it and paused outside trying to hear.

He couldn't make out a thing going on inside. Silently and gently he turned the knob on the door. It twisted fully, then he eased the door back. It moved. Good, not locked. He edged the door open an inch so he could look through.

Yes, he could see the back room of the mining-equipment store. He couldn't see the storeowner. He opened the door another inch and now spotted the retailer near the front curtain, tied to a chair. A man O'Grady hadn't seen stood near him, a six-gun in his hand, but it wasn't pointing at Gathers.

A moment later he heard the front door burst open and someone run inside.

"No, no, don't kill my father," Nita screamed. "Please, don't hurt him. I couldn't find that man you wanted."

The man near Gathers looked toward the front, then walked to the curtained doorway and went through.

The moment he moved, so did O'Grady. On silent feet he slipped in the partly opened door and strode toward the gunman. O'Grady had his six-gun up and ready.

Four feet from the other man, O'Grady's foot made a board squeak in the floor. The man whirled just in time to take a slashing blow from the side of the Colt down across his forehead. He looked up in surprise, then crumpled toward the floor. O'Grady caught him and eased him down. He took the gun from him and quickly bound his hands with a piece of rope that lay near where Gathers was tied.

O'Grady looked at Gathers and held a finger across his lips. Gathers saw this, nodded, and said nothing. O'Grady cut Gathers loose and handed him the kidnapper's gun. Slowly they both moved toward the curtain.

They heard the girl screaming and arguing with Loonin in the store.

As they parted the curtain, O'Grady saw them standing about four feet apart. Loonin didn't have a gun. His left hand must not be good with one, and his right wrist and arm sported a white plaster cast. O'Grady stepped through the drape and aimed at the Moudry's gunman.

"Hold it, Loonin, or you're dead," O'Grady barked.

The man turned and stared for a moment, then he dived toward the girl.

O'Grady fired. The lead slug hit Loonin in the right leg before he got to Nita, and spilled him against a display of shovels. The round exploding in the closed store sounded like a battery of artillery going off all at once. Loonin crashed to the floor and grabbed a shovel with his left hand.

"Drop it, Loonin, or I'll put another hole in you."

Loonin let go of the shovel and Nita ran to her father.

O'Grady walked up to Loonin. "Heard you wanted to talk to me, Loonin. Anything important?"

"I'm bleeding to death! Fix my damn leg."

"Why? Been days and days since I watched a man bleed to death. Not a bad way to go. You get weaker and weaker, then they tell me the mind starts to wander as the blood supply to the brain thins out. Your hands and feet will get numb first, then you won't be able to move them. In another minute or so your brain will be starved for blood and you'll go into convulsions, or just get sleepy and fade into eternity. Sound like fun, Loonin?''

"Yeah, yeah, I get the picture. If I talk, you'll tie up my leg. What the hell you want to know?''

"You work for Moudry, right?''

"Yes.''

"You want to know what I'm doing in town?''

"Yes. Now tie up my leg. I can't do it.''

"Have you killed anyone on Moudry's orders?'' O'Grady asked.

Loonin looked away.

"You don't have to answer, I know you have. How did you kill Luke Denker, the mine inspector? Did you shoot him or bash him on the head with a drill?''

"Who?''

"Luke Denker, the guy you buried at the hundred-foot level in the Bonanza.''

"Don't know what you're talking about.''

O'Grady looked down at the blood that seeped through Loonin's fingers as he tried to stop it coming from his leg. "Blood sure is red, isn't it? Look how it puddles on the floor under your leg. I figure it'll run about six feet before you get numb.''

"Oh, damn, that hurts. Get me to the doctor.''

"You talk, Loonin, then we'll walk.''

"Okay, so I push some people around now and then. Nobody ever convicted me of killing nobody. You can't either.''

"Don't have to,'' O'Grady said. He pulled his six-gun from leather and cocked it. The sound of metal sliding back on metal and catching jolted like a death knell in the store. A customer looked in the open front door, changed his mind, and walked away.

"You wouldn't,'' Loonin said.

"Why not? I know you killed Denker, half the town

knows you killed him. You know you killed him. You're guilty of murder, you need to be executed. I'm an executioner—only I do it with a gun, not a rope. You ready?''

Loonin wiped sweat from his forehead; a drop skittered down his cheek. "Look, we can talk about this."

O'Grady brought the muzzle up and from six feet away aimed at Loonin's left eye. "What's to talk about? The talking time is past."

"Okay, okay! I did it. Killed Denker. Moudry made me. I'm just saying this so you won't kill me."

"I know, not worth a damn in court. I'll bandage you up some and then we're going to see your boss."

"Moudry? He'll kill me." Loonin's face paled, his left hand began to shake. "Don't take me to see him, don't!"

"Best reason I've heard so far," O'Grady said. "We're making some progress here." As O'Grady tied up Loonin's leg to stop the bleeding, he sent Gathers to see if he could find Marshal Jones. "When you find him, charge that goon in your back room with assault and battery, with attempted murder, with kidnapping and conspiracy. That should hold him for the territorial judge."

O'Grady lifted Loonin to his feet. "Now, little man, let's march up to see Moudry."

They walked the quarter of a mile to the Bonanza shaft and mine office. Workmen pounded nails on the third floor. Loonin limped badly by the time he made it to the front door of the office. He pushed it open, stumbled in, and leaned against the wall.

"Canyon O'Grady and friend to see Mr. Moudry," O'Grady said to the startled office worker. The man, who wore a green eyeshade and garters holding up his blue-striped dress-shirt sleeves, looked at a door across the way.

"Never mind," O'Grady said. "We'll introduce ourselves." He prodded Loonin forward to the door the clerk had looked at and turned the knob and pushed it inward. O'Grady pushed Loonin forward. He hit on his shot leg and stumbled, then fell into the thick carpet on the office floor.

The Bonanza king had just started wiping his tearing eyes when the two men burst into the room. He saw them, finished wiping his eyes, and kept his hands in plain sight.

"Edwin Moudry, my name is Canyon O'Grady and I'm returning some of your garbage. You're not overly particular about who you hire to do your work."

"I haven't the least idea what you're talking about. This man is one of more than thirty guards I employ around my mines."

O'Grady snorted, then roared with laughter. "That's a damn silly response, Moudry. I expected something just a whole lot better out of you. A nice bald-faced lie, or maybe something completely outrageous. One of your guards? That's just stupid."

The small man stood slowly, his eyes furious. Twice he started to speak, but couldn't. He took deep breaths to calm himself. Then he swallowed three or four times and tried again. "Get out. No man calls me stupid."

"I do. You're stupid if you think you can get away with murder. And that's exactly what you're trying. I'm putting you on notice, Moudry: I'm coming after your hide. You so much as spit on the boardwalk and I'll have you charged with a crime. Understand?"

Edwin A. Moudry's round, fleshy face turned red and he pointed at the door. He couldn't say a word.

O'Grady picked up Loonin, pushed him toward the desk, then bent him down on top of the big surface.

"Here's your current killer, Moudry. In this territory, if you hire a man to kill another, the law says you're as guilty as the man who pulls the trigger. Remember that. If you're thinking of cashing in my chips, remember this: I've made a complete deposition with the U.S. marshal and the territorial judge. I've told them about Loonin, my charges against you, and my accusation against you if I turn up dead. You'll be tried and hung within three or four hours."

O'Grady turned and walked out the door, his broad, unprotected back showing his disdain for their danger to him.

Halfway back down the mountain to C Street, Marshal Ben Jones waited for O'Grady.

"No blood?" the lawman asked. "That prisoner Gathers brought me had a little running off his face."

"Some more on Rush Loonin. He tried to get frisky again. Man developed a hole in his leg. Strange how it happened."

"And you delivered him back to Moudry bleeding like a sieve."

"Bleeding some. Gave the man a challenge. Told him that I knew he killed Luke Denker and that I was going to prove it. He was so shook up he couldn't even speak for a minute or two. He's an emotional man, this Moudry is."

O'Grady told the marshal about his statement to Moudry about the deposition with the marshal naming Moudry as the prime suspect in case of O'Grady's sudden demise.

"How did he take it?"

"Love to play poker with that guy. He can't read a bluff any better than my horse."

"I'll let you know the next time we play." They walked on down the hill to C Street. "You talked to Orrin yet?"

"No. Orrin who?"

"Quedenfeld. Orrin Quedenfeld, he's our saddle-maker."

"He's here in town?"

"Sure is. I'm going that way, I'll introduce you."

"He's not one of Moudry's boys, I'd guess."

"You're right, O'Grady. He's about as far from that as you are. He's over there, next to the tannery. He owns that place too. Brings in raw hides from all over."

They came to the saddle shop and the marshal went in first.

A host of glorious smells assailed O'Grady as soon as they entered the shop. Leather in all its pungent, nose-grabbing qualities, a scent unlike any other, and one that O'Grady had always loved from the moment he tried to make a belt out of a long strip of cowhide.

"Well, Orrin, I see you've almost got that one done," Marshal Jones said. "This the same saddle you were working on last week?"

The man working on a saddle on a stand turned. He was black, about thirty-five or so. His face broke into a strong smile. "Marshal Jones, you old polecat. This is a brand-new saddle, can't you see the difference? Now, who is this gentleman with you?"

They looked back at O'Grady.

"This is a new friend of mine, an Irishman of many talents by the name of Canyon O'Grady."

The black man held out his hand and O'Grady took it. That was when O'Grady looked at the saddle-maker's eyes. There was a thin white film over both of them. The saddler was blind.

7

Canyon O'Grady shook the saddle-maker's hand firmly and then let go. He was surprised. How did a blind man make saddles?

Orrin Quedenfeld laughed gently. "Yes, sir, here is a man well in control of himself. Not a glimmer of a tremble when he at last figured out I was blind. I always like to meet people for the first time and judge their reactions."

"You couldn't have been more right this time," Marshal Jones said. "O'Grady here never even blinked when he figured you out. Now, to the important thing. Is that bottomless coffeepot of yours empty yet?"

"Not by a damn sight," Orrin said. "If I may use that word. I'll pour." He moved surely through his shop, maneuvering around two turns to a small wood cook stove where a pot of coffee sat heating over a banked fire fed by split pine sticks.

All three cups were full when Orrin brought them back. He handed one to each man, then swung his leg over the saddle he was working on, and sat.

"Feel right?" O'Grady asked. "I've heard that the best saddle-makers won't let one out of their shop until it feels right when they sit it."

"Can't feel finished-right yet, 'cause it ain't finished, but it's coming along. O'Grady. Irish red hair and everything?"

"Depends on what you mean by everything."

"The temperament, the fine tenor voice, and the fierce loyalty to back up a hair-trigger temper." Orrin grinned. "Hey, I'm not insulting the Irish. I find all of those qualities admirable."

"From what I've seen of him in a day and a half, I'd say he has a good portion of all of those attributes," Marshal Jones said. "But, hell, we all can't be perfect."

The three men laughed.

"O'Grady is asking questions about Luke Denker," Marshal Jones said.

"Damn and double damn," Orrin said. He stepped out of the saddle and moved two feet to his waist-high workbench where he had been forming a leather skirt over two feet long for the saddle. "I knew the man for six months. Hard to find a nicer gentleman, a better human being. Somebody killed him."

"You know that for sure, Orrin?"

"As near as a man can without having any facts. Luke caught in a mine cave-in? Rubbish. He knew more about mines than anyone on the mountain. He was a hard rock-mine tunnel inspector. He wouldn't even look into a tunnel if he figured it wasn't safe. Saying he was caught in a cave-in is like saying a saddle-maker died because he sewed his nose shut to a saddle."

"Who?" Marshal Jones asked.

"Who?" Orrin asked with disdain. "One man. The Bonanza mine-owner gave the order, and one of his killers did the job. Luke told me the night before he died that the Bonanza just started tunneling along a vein from the coyote hole. They had put in the first twenty feet of tunnel and they hadn't put in their square sets right. Square sets are beams fit just so that hold up the roof of a tunnel or the roof of a whole damn room underground. He said he was gonna make them tear it all out and do it right or he'd close down the mine."

"You never told me that before, Orrin," Jones said.

"No need. Now Washington sends out a man to dig into it." He grinned again and raised his hands to halt Canyon's protest. "O'Grady, you have to be a federal man of some kind. Nobody else gonna be looking into Luke's death. He told me he was the last Denker in his line. So no family's going to be checking up on him. Our fine Irish tenor here has to be a federal man. But all I know is what he told me. And that isn't evidence. Nothing I could testify before the territorial judge, is it?"

"Not courtroom evidence, but it'll be a help to me," O'Grady said.

"Hope so." Orrin used a razor-sharp knife and neatly cut along a scroll mark to form the skirt. It would have triple stitching around it before he was done, and it'd be lined with sheepskin wool. He felt the cut, shaved off a place that was slightly out of line, and laid it aside.

"Who would Luke have made the inspection tour with at the Bonanza when he told them what they had to do?" O'Grady asked.

"Said he was going to insist that Edwin Moudry himself come down. Moudry has been a hard-rock miner for years. He knows the shafts and tunnels."

"Damn," Jones said.

"Double that," O'Grady said. "We've got a murder, we know who did it—or at least who ordered it done—and we can't prove it. The man is going to walk away free and clear."

"Unless somebody catches up with him," Orrin said. "But nobody in this town will do it. They're all

56

thinking big money, big wide silver veins worth four thousand dollars a ton. Why worry about one mine inspector?"

"Orrin, was Luke the one you played chess with?" Marshal Jones asked.

"One game after work every night except Sunday. He was ahead in our match eighty-six games to eighty-two."

"You play chess, too?" O'Grady said, surprised.

"Of course. My own set. You promise not to cheat, I'll challenge you to a game. Speaking of playing instruments, Julia has one little girl I can play like a fine fiddle."

The men laughed and sipped at their coffee.

"So, Mr. O'Grady, you come up to a blank wall on the Denker murder?" Orrin asked, concern returning to his face.

"Hell, no. Just getting started. Is the Bonanza worth anything? Is it going to make Moudry a millionaire?"

Orrin shrugged. "Don't know."

Marshal Jones scowled for a minute. "The mining people I know say there's no way to tell. First men here scraped the gold off the top and threw away the blue mud. That blue mud was rich, rich silver ore. Now the surface traces of the silver are gone and they're following the veins into the mountain." He stood and walked around the leather shop, touching the leather, staring at the nearly finished saddle. "Some mining engineers tell me there could be a vein of silver ore a hundred feet wide down there someplace. Whoever finds it first is a millionaire a dozen times over."

"Finding that big vein is the rub," Orrin said. "One miner I know had to sell his claim because he didn't have enough money to dig down to even find out if there was a vein on his claim.''

"It's a big business around here buying and selling mining claims," the marshal said. "Kind of like gambling. Lots of men made a claim, panned some gold or dug a little silver, and sold the ore to someone; then they ran out of money and sold a fifty-foot claim for a hundred dollars, or five hundred dollars.''

Orrin nodded. "O'Grady, you met Elly yet, down at the Beanery? Hell, she was here when it all started. She had a little boardinghouse and she'd give credit to the gold-mine panners when they was down on their luck. When the silver came in and all these old friends staked out claims, some of them settled up with Elly by giving her ten feet of a claim.

"People said Elly had as many as eight or ten little chunks of claims around the mountain. Lots of folks sold out those first claims dirt cheap, and they might rue the day. If just one of them strips comes in with a good-size silver vein, Elly will be so rich she can buy half the town.''

"The more I know about this town, the better,'' O'Grady said. "Orrin you've probably heard me shuffling my feet here a little. I'm getting ready to thank you for the coffee. I've got to get down to the stables and check on my horse.''

"Hope you didn't ride all the way from Washington, D.C., O'Grady," Marshal Jones said.

"Note quite. Wherever I go, I try to get my palomino on board a train. This time I was lucky and got him into an empty box car. Then I rode up here from the last stop.''

"Palomino?" Orrin asked. "Is that the one that's copper-toned and with a pure white mane and tail?''

"That's the kind. Not a lot of them around, and I wouldn't trade a private rail car for this one. Well, I might. He's gonna bite my hand off if I don't go down and give him a run. He would much prefer an open pasture to a stall, but right now that's the best we can do."

"Good meeting you, Mr. O'Grady. Don't forget about that chess game. That's how I go to sleep, lay there picturing the board and working out new attacks. Oh, damn. I gave away my whole strategy. I love to attack, not defend."

"I'll be back, Orrin, you can count on it."

Outside, the lawman and O'Grady walked toward the far end of C Street, where the first livery had been erected and part of the town had grown around it. Nobody thought to ask the owner to move it.

"Mind if I walk along? Don't remember seeing a palomino. Yours is a stallion?"

"Right. His name is Cormack, after a great Irish king."

In the stable, Cormack whinnied when he saw O'Grady. He curried the horse and brushed him down, examined all four hooves and shoes; then he put on a bridle, a saddle blanket, and the big western saddle and led him out.

"Going for a ride?"

"Just a little workout for Cormack, he needs it. Gives me some thinking time. Wish I knew what to do with Moudry. He acted about the way I guessed he would when I confronted him."

"Remember, that card you carry doesn't give you a license to kill. Legally we can't touch him," the marshal said.

"But if I can get him mad enough to come after me himself and he shoots first, then I've got a right to defend myself. That might work. Trouble is he knows the same thing." O'Grady tightened up both cinch straps on the saddle, then stepped on board.

"Remember, no hunting license. You get any solid evidence against the man, I want to be the first to know."

"You will be, Marshal. The first, after me." Canyon waved and nudged the big stallion out the walkway and out the front gate. He rode to the end of the row of buildings of C Street. When they petered out, he cut up across the flank of Mount Davidson, then angled back to C Street, which had become a wagon trail, and rode a half-mile farther out of the settlement.

The bronze-and-golden coat of the big animal rippled as he galloped along for a while, blasting along as fast as he could go. Then O'Grady slowed him down, turned around, and walked him back toward the livery.

Nobody shot at him. The only two riders he passed waved and kept going toward Carson City.

At the livery, he unsaddled Cormack, rubbed him down, and gave him a long drink at the watering trough. O'Grady treated the big lad to three pounds of oats and headed back toward the hotel. He stopped instead at Gathers' store and found Nita minding the front.

He saw her long blond hair as soon as he stepped in the door. There were no customers.

She stepped around the counter and smiled. "I'm glad to see you again." She seemed relieved. "I was fearful that Mr. Moudry had hurt you up there."

"No such luck." He looked at the big clock on the wall. "Almost noontime. Have you had your dinner yet?"

She shook her head, and the shoulder-length blond hair swirled.

"Then why don't I take you out to dinner? You pick the best place in town. It'll be for giving me such a good supper last night."

She frowned for a moment, then smiled. "Yes. I'll tell Father I'm going. I would really like to have a chance to talk to you."

8

Their noon meal at the New Delmonico went well, O'Grady thought. He had a thick steak and Nita ate some French dish that he didn't even try to pronounce.

Nita looked up and brushed a strand of blond hair out of her eyes. "Canyon O'Grady, I want to ask a favor. I know there's nobody else in town who can do this job. I want you to do it. You're about my last hope. Please stop Father from writing those articles about the dangers of working in the Bonanza. It's going to get him killed, and I just won't stand for that!"

Canyon wanted to grin, she was so upset, so furious, but at the same time so damned cute. He kept a straight face. "I understand. But your father is a strong and a proud man. I can't go up and tell him not to worry about the other miners, and not to grieve for his dead son. It's all wrapped up together." He lowered his voice and moved slightly closer to her. "I'm working on something that might change the management of the Bonanza Mine. Can't promise anything, but there's a chance."

She reached out and touched his hand, covered it with both of hers on the table. "I'm so glad. It's something to hope for." Her blue eyes glowed, her smile glorious. "You know you're probably saving my father's life . . . again."

"My pleasure, especially when it produces a great smile like that. How's the dinner?"

"Oh, I haven't even noticed. I'm so worried about Father. I'm sure it's good. I'll be quiet now and let you eat."

They had just finished the meal when O'Grady saw Rush Loonin start into the dining room. He stopped near the door and stared hard at O'Grady and the girl. For a moment his face took on a sly grin, then he backed out of the small entryway and hurried up the street in the direction of the Bonanza.

O'Grady thought nothing more about it. At least he wouldn't have another showdown with the man. It was plain that Loonin still worked for Moudry and was probably on his way to report O'Grady's location. Moudry would make another attempt to kill him, O'Grady was sure. He just didn't know the time or the place . . . or the method. It wouldn't be a hundred feet underground in Mount Davidson, he was damn sure of that.

When they finished their coffee, O'Grady paid the tab and they walked the short block back to the mining-equipment store.

Gathers grinned when he saw them. "Well, how was dinner? Did Nita try to talk you into getting me to stop writing my articles?"

"She tried. I told her you were too stubborn to be convinced. Am I right?"

"Absolutely. I'm too stubborn to live, but I'd like to, for a while yet."

"Good, Gathers. Make you a deal. You hold up writing another article and give me a week to put a stop to the major problem, which you seem to think is Edwin A. Moudry. Is it a deal?"

"Hey, I thought you were on my side," the merchant ranted.

"I am. I have some plans for Mr. Moudry myself and I don't want you messing them up. Is it a deal? What do you have to lose? Either way you'll be getting rid of Moudry."

The merchant cut a wire holding six drifting picks together and marked the price on each one. In a normal town they would sell for forty-five cents. Up here the price was two dollars each. Gathers shrugged. "Hell, why not? If both of you want me to hold off awhile, I've got plenty of work to do around here. Just so Nita runs the change drawer for me."

"I'll be glad to, Daddy."

O'Grady motioned the merchant out to the back dock on the alley. "I been wondering about something else. You know something about this mining town. Is this just a flash in the pan, or is this silver mining going to last? What if they find no more veins and the ones they got run out?"

"Been known to happen in every mining strike ever made, O'Grady, you must know that. Could happen here tomorrow."

"What are the odds, the potential of the area? What I need to know is, is Virginia City and the Comstock really going to hit it big? This $4,791-to-the-ton ore with two-thirds in silver might never show up again. If it's a shattered vein and worth twenty dollars a ton, somebody will mine it. But the question is this: is there a hundred-foot-wide vein of pure silver down there in the mountain five hundred or a thousand feet, and if it's there is, will anyone go down to find it?"

Gathers pounded a shovel against the dock. "You know I've done some mining. Placer for gold and some hard-rock work. I got out of it. Not steady. A store is. The Comstock Lode? It might be a quick hit-and-run. Might not be a soul here digging silver in another year. Then again, there might be twenty thousand people here for thirty years and everyone getting filthy, stinking rich.''

''So it's a question without an answer?''

''No, but the answer has to be a maybe. From the ore I've seen and some of the veins of silver I've watched followed underground, I'd venture a guess that this is the real thing. There might be some lean years as one vein runs out and before another one or two or three are found, but I'd say this is the place. How much?'' Adolph Gathers looked down the alley and into the distance. His eyes grew misty and he shook his head. ''My guess is that over the next twenty years, there will be over three hundred million dollars taken out of the ground in this area, most of it from the right here inside of Mount Davidson.''

O'Grady stared at him. ''That's a lot of silver.''

''There's a lot of silver down there, somewhere. I can feel it, smell it, but I'm not going to try to find it. I'm past that phase of my life. Some of these men walking around town right now without a shovel to their name will wind up as accidental millionaires.''

''Thanks for your prediction. I hope it's right. Now I better get about some business. I'll say good-bye to Nita.'' He went inside and left Gathers digging into some supplies on the dock.

Nita stood by the small counter near the cash drawer. There were no customers in the store. She looked up and smiled. ''Thanks for getting Father to stop writing those articles.''

''For a little while at least,'' O'Grady said. He noticed the sleek way she fit into her dress, which covered her neck to shoe tops, but allowed for the tight swell of her breasts. She walked up to him.

''I did think of something I could do to thank you,'' Nita said. She reached up and kissed his lips, a solid, firm, and lingering kiss that brought a quick reaction from him. She moved her lips off his and waited.

He reached around her and pulled her small form hard against him and claimed her lips in another hard, passionate kiss. When he eased away from her, Nita still had her eyes closed. She opened them and found him watching her. Gently he let go of her and she stepped back.

"I know I'm brazen and wanton, but I've been wanting to kiss you ever since that first night."

"Good. I always enjoy kissing a beautiful lady."

Nita watched him. "Can you . . . I mean, could you stop by tonight, for supper or afterward? We could . . . talk, play dominoes, maybe."

"I'll try, but I can't promise I'll be there. I have several more men to talk to."

"I understand." She moved back so he could walk past her; as he did, she touched his arm. He looked down at her. "Canyon, I enjoyed those kisses, both of them." She turned before he could reply and walked toward the back of the store.

O'Grady did have more people to see. Jones had told him that Seth Kearney was one of the shrewdest claim-traders in Virginia City. He had been here since the start, and had owed Elly Handshoe three pieces of claims to settle up his back board bill. He not only paid up but now owned dozens of parcels. He had a small office across from the saddle shop. O'Grady turned the knob and walked inside.

The office was eight feet square with no other door. The room was made of raw lumber without paint or wallpaper or plaster. The floorboards were the same sawed green pine planks that had shrunken when they dried, leaving gaps a person could lose a pocketknife through.

The desk had once been two packing boxes with

slabs of two-by-sixes nailed to them and what looked like the felt from a well-used pool table tacked over the top.

Behind the desk sat a man with frizzled blond hair. Half of it stood straight up from his skull, some slanted down the back of his head, and some strayed toward his ears. He wore spectacles and concentrated so hard on a claim map in front of him that he didn't hear O'Grady come inside.

The government agent cleared his throat and stepped up to the desk.

"What? Oh, yes, I didn't hear you come in." Seth Kearney was about forty. He looked like he spent every waking hour thinking about claims, and buying and selling them.

"You have a claim to sell?" Kearney blinked and looked again at his visitor. "No? Excuse me, you would be wanting to buy. I recently came into the control of three fifty-foot claims in a row. Make a delicious gamble for anyone with only three thousand dollars."

"Sorry, I'm not that much of a gambler. I would like to talk to you, if you have some time."

"Talk about mining, about the Comstock Lode?"

"Yes, absolutely."

"Good. You one of them newspapermen snooping around?"

"Afraid not. I'm looking for an estimate of how much silver there is in Mount Davidson and in the Washoe River area."

Seth Kearney guffawed. He looked at O'Grady and roared in laughter until tears came streaming down his cheeks. Kearney backed away from his desk and slapped his thigh in delight. He hooted and roared and guffawed for at least two minutes before he could get himself under control.

"You must be from out of town and you're using this method trying to decide whether to invest in mining stock or in a mine itself." He wiped his eyes, blew his nose on a white rag and gave a big sigh, getting himself totally under control. "Excuse me, but I haven't had that good a laugh in six months. You and everyone else wants to know how much silver is in the Comstock. Nobody will tell you because nobody knows. I'd be glad to tell you if I could. All of the veins aren't going to assay out to forty-seven, ninety-one a ton. All of the veins aren't going to outcrop where we can find them easily. But it's down there. The big trouble is raising the money to dig down and find the silver."

"I've heard a figure of three hundred million. Is that possible?"

"Of course, possible. Probable, I don't know. Look at this claim." Kearney stabbed a finger at a small square on the claim map. "Not a hundred yards from the Ophir Mine is a coyote hole down nearly a hundred and twenty feet with six tunnels off it, and they ain't uncovered a spade full of silver ore. Over a hundred yards away the Ophir is taking out a thousand a day. A gamble, a damn big gamble. But, my friend, if you win, you get wined and dined by the crown heads of Europe."

"How many will win big here?"

"A dozen, maybe. Ten, fourteen, who knows? Just depends how deep they can go. On one hard-rock gold mine I worked they figured they found only about one ounce of gold for every five hundred ounces that were in the mountain. Trouble was the veins went straight down in spots, and in others places they shattered like a whiskey bottle over a drunk's head, taking off in all directions. Mining is a crazy business."

"So, I want to ask you again, is this a big one, a real El Dorado?"

Kearney looked at him with one eye squinted shut. "What the hell difference does it make to you? You aren't buying in. You aren't investing. You aren't digging. Hell, you probably won't even stay around to find out if what I say happens or not." He stood and hobbled to the window and looked out. One of his legs seemed to be stiff at the knee.

"Yeah, yeah, old mining accident. I'm really a miner, not a damn lawyer. Rather be down there on the tunnel face socking some holes in the slab to muck out the ore. But here I am stuck on the topside just listening to the men who come up."

He wiped one hand over his face and then hobbled back to his desk with obvious pain. He sat down and sighed. "Well, hell. You must have some good reason for asking the questions. Yeah, I think this is a big one. I've been waiting all my life, and to me this has to be it. I missed the forty-niner. This has got to be it for me. You know that already three of the four good strikes are incorporated and selling stock in San Francisco. Takes a whole piss pot full of money to do silver mining. That means lawsuits. So far I've made ten times as much as a lawyer on lawsuits about claims than I ever dug out of a mine. This is just the start. I play my cards right and I'll make a million as a lawyer."

He sighed again, stared back at the map of patchwork plots on the map on his desk. "Yes, young man, I'd say this is big, the El Dorado the likes of which this nation will never know again. Should call this Silver Mountain. Hell, I know that there is more silver in this mountain than this country has ever seen.

"If I'm right, or if I'm wrong, I'm still a rich man on the lawsuits." He grinned. "Now that I've cleansed my soul, sure you aren't interested in a splinter of a claim? I've got a nice little ten-foot section on Gold Hill that I can let you have for $379. The owner's mother died in Chicago and he's got to get back there for the funeral.''

''Mr. Kearney, I appreciate your offer, but I'm financially embarrassed right now. I'll certainly keep the parcel in mind. I also thank you for your estimate of the total value of this area's mining potential.''

A man opened the outside door and stomped in. He was a miner with mud on his boots and a ragged shirt over his shoulder. He wore no hat and he had a week's growth of beard.

''Hey, Seth, you buy that claim I want?''

''Not so far, Will. I'm trying.''

''Double the offer, but do it in gradual amounts. I know he wants to sell. He's got trouble with his wife back in Sacramento. Another week's all I got.'' The man closed the door and was gone.

''One of my buyers. He's got a claim next to this one and thinks he's about ready to hit a vein. Of course, this is confidential, you understand.''

''Of course.'' O'Grady exited.

He took a tour up the mountain, looking at every dig, every coyote-hole shaft sunk into the ground. The men were excited or dead tired, enthused or morose. It was backbreaking work here, now that the surface riches were gone.

''Hell, I'm a placer miner,'' one youth told him. ''I'd rather pan a stream than go down in some damned rat hole in the ground.''

O'Grady stayed away from the big mines, and at about five o'clock he headed back to C Street and then on to the Gathers' house. Maybe he could watch Nita get supper. He figured he had about half of his work done here in Virginia City.

He arrived at the house at the same time Adolph did. They went in the front door together.

"Nita, guess who is here with me?" Gathers called as he hung his hat on the wall rack. There was no answer. They went to the kitchen and saw that no supper was in the process of cooking.

"What the hell?" Gathers said.

O'Grady saw a piece of paper on the kitchen table. He grabbed it and read out loud, " 'Gathers: We have your daughter. Only way you'll ever see her again is to do exactly what we tell you to do.' "

"Oh, God! They've kidnapped Nita," Gathers said, and he sat down quickly in the kitchen chair.

9

Adolph Gathers stared at O'Grady from the chair where he had collapsed when he heard that Nita had been kidnapped. "Read the rest of it," he said softly.

" 'You must do the following: first don't tell anyone about this, especially not the marshal or Canyon O'Grady. Second, tell O'Grady someone wants to meet him at a small flat place on the mountain about a quarter of a mile uphill from the Bonanza Mine buildings. Be sure he's there just at dusk today. Third, get five hundred dollars in cash and have O'Grady bring it with him to ransom Nita. Don't tell him what's in the package or about the kidnapping. Fourth, be sure he rides that palomino of his. Fifth, swear that you will never write another article for the newspaper here or elsewhere about conditions in the mines of Virginia City. If any of these conditions are not met, the only way you'll ever see your daughter again will be in a coffin.' "

Gathers was staring out the window.

"There's no signature, Gathers," Canyon said. "Somebody is serious about this."

"Two hours until dusk. What are we going to do?"

"We're going to do exactly as they say. Only what happens when I get there won't be what they want to happen."

Gathers shook his head, went to the basin on the

72

counter, washed his face in cold water, and dried it off with a hand towel. "Damn, I been afraid of something like this. Nita was my weak spot. But why you? Unless . . . yeah. I should have seen it before. A damn stupid ransom note. They want to shut me up, but at the same time they want five hundred dollars cash and they want you there so they can murder you and take your palomino. The bastards!"

"About the size of them, laddie. But don't worry, we'll have some surprise for them. You have a shotgun and a hacksaw?"

Gathers grinned. "Damn right, and I know exactly where to cut off the barrels. It's a twin-barreled ten-gauge. Blow a horse right out of its shoes if you get close enough."

"You fix it and dig out a dozen rounds. I'll go get Cormack and a long black duster traveling coat."

"Good. I'm feeling better already."

Twenty minutes later O'Grady rode Cormack up to the back door of the Gathers home and stepped down. He patted the golden shoulder of the stallion and talked to him, then tied him to the back porch and went inside.

Gathers looked up. "Sawed them off, filed off the burrs, and got her in shape. She's been used, but is smooth as a silk shirt."

O'Grady took the weapon and cracked it open. The barrels were free of any burrs inside from the hacksawing. He snapped it closed and pulled it up to his waist.

"Feels good. Sometimes they get cut off too short. This is just right."

Adolph gave him a small cloth bag filled with shotgun shells. It had a narrow cloth strap to go over his shoulder. A hunters's helper.

"You're taking a rifle, too, I'd guess," Gathers said.

"True, a Henry that can throw out thirteen shots without reloading the tube."

"Good. I fixed you some grub, ham sandwiches. Made half a dozen for you to take with you, 'case this extends at all. Nita's gonna be hungry too. Sit down and have some coffee and some beans and bacon to get you off to a good start. I guess you want to get out there early. There's no cover along that section of the mountain."

"Figures. I'll be there, let them know I'm coming, and then hope I'm guessing right. They want an open shot at me, so I'll have to play it smart."

He ate, drank a second cup of coffee, and stepped into the saddle. He had changed clothes and now wore a pair of denim trail pants, a blue shirt and leather vest, and his low-crowned brown hat.

He rode to the end of C Street that angled toward the Bonanza. When he came to the end of the track, he cut north into the side of the mountain and rode a half-mile past the Bonanza buildings, then began to climb. He saw two men outside the mine offices watching his direction. Both had rifles. He kicked off the mount and walked up the hill so Cormack was between him and the gunmen.

They wanted Cormack, so they wouldn't risk hitting the horse on the chance they might hit the man behind him.

This way, O'Grady worked up past the level spot. It looked like it had been made by tailings from some tunnel dug into the side of the mountain. Now it was level and well-weathered from wind, rain, and snow.

Fifty yards from the level spot he found what he had been looking for, a jumble of rocks and some granite upthrusts that were big enough to hide both him and Cormack. He moved in there, tied the palomino to a scrub of sage, and looked for a firing position.

If it was going to be a war, he had to be ready. The sawed-off shotgun and the sack of shells bumped reassuringly against him under the duster, which came well below his knees. The two men by the mine buildings probably knew he had a rifle. They didn't know about the shotgun.

He found the spot he wanted. Two rocks met forming a small V that was big enough to take the barrel of the Henry. It also was wide enough to let the long rifle rest there without being held. An ideal firing position. He could sit behind the weapon and be entirely protected except when he lifted up to shoot.

O'Grady looked at the sun. It had just vanished behind the side of a mountain, and already the feathers of darkness began to devour the daylight.

It was still light enough ten minutes later so he could see two horses coming toward the level spot from the mine area. One had a large rider, the other a smaller one. Could be Nita, but probably wasn't. It would be a small man with a shotgun.

O'Grady watched them ride slowly up the hill to the flat place and both get off their mounts. He couldn't tell anything about the smaller one, but he still guessed the person was not Nita.

"O'Grady. We know you're up there. Watched you ride in. Come on down with the money and we'll make the trade. The cash for the girl. Sounds fair."

O'Grady didn't recognize the voice. The man stood there watching the rocks. Then the government agent realized the smaller mine man still had a hat on.

"Tell Nita to take off her hat," O'Grady bellowed at the pair. There was a hasty conversation below, then both men jumped on their horses. O'Grady cut down the larger man just as he hit the saddle. He jolted off the mount with a slug through his shoulder, and his suddenly free horse galloped off.

The federal agent levered in a new round and sighted toward the smaller man, then moved the aim and slammed the round into the man's horse's head. It went down, dead before it hit the ground. The man rolled free and started to run.

A slug bit into the rocks in front of the fleeing figure, and he stopped and held up both hands. "Okay, it didn't work," the man said.

"Drop your gun belt, then move back to your buddy and take his." Just then O'Grady heard a slight movement to one side and spun that way, his shot coming a fraction of a second before that of the wounded man who had sat up and cocked his six-gun.

The mine man's slug ripped into the ground to the left of O'Grady, but the agent's well-aimed shot caught the gunman in the chest, slamming him backward, taking him to hell in a fraction of a second.

O'Grady looked back at the unwounded rider, who had thrown off the long cape he wore. His six-gun and belt lay on the ground at his feet.

"You gonna kill me, too?"

"I should. Who sent you up here?"

"Loonin. He said for sure you'd come."

"I did. Where is he?"

"Gone to the cabin."

"What cabin?"

"One he used now and again over in Witch Creek Canyon, about two miles over where there's a nice mess of pine trees."

"Sit down," O'Grady told the man. "Then lay down on your face in the sand."

"You aiming to kill me, O'Grady?"

"You knew who you were trying to kill?"

"Yeah, Loonin told us."

"If I wanted you dead, you'd be in hell by now. Lay down and shut up." O'Grady jogged back to the out-

76

cropping in the now nearly full dark and mounted Cormack. He rode the palomino out of the rocks and moved up slowly on the dead man's horse where it sniffed at the dry weeds thirty yards away from the body.

O'Grady caught the mount's reins and led her back to the prone man. "Get on," the agent ordered.

When the ambusher was in the saddle, O'Grady tied his left hand securely to the saddle horn with a strip of rawhide from his saddlebags. "What's your first name?"

"George."

"Do you feel lucky, George?"

"I hope so."

"Good. If you're lucky, you can find that cabin in the dark. That's where Loonin took the girl?"

"Yes, sir. Told us he was gunna, and we saw him ride off with her."

"You better be telling the truth, George. It's the only way you're going to stay alive."

They rode.

It was nearly an hour and a half later when they came into a stand of dry land pines—ponderosa, O'Grady figured. There was a small, almost dry watercourse maybe two feet wide.

"In the spring runoff and after rains, this is a fair-sized little crick," George said.

"Shut up, George. The cabin upstream?"

"Yeah, maybe a half-mile."

The narrow little canyon became tighter and tighter as they rode. A hundred yards later O'Grady smelled smoke. He stopped, untied George, and put him on the ground, then tied him hand and foot and picketed the horse a dozen feet away.

"Can you stay quiet or should I gag you?"

"I'll be quiet. Damn, I know when I'm beat."

77

"You're damn well beaten, George. Don't forget it." O'Grady vanished in the darkness. He moved forward slowly, so he wouldn't make a sound. Twice he stopped for a full minute and listened. Nothing. He moved again.

He saw the cabin a few minutes later looming out of the black-on-black background. It could have been there for twenty years. One side had fallen in, but the rest looked solid enough in the gloom.

A small light showed through one window that had been long broken out and covered with a flapping piece of an old blanket.

O'Grady invested another five minutes moving up slowly on the window. At last he edged his eyes past the window frame and looked in the cabin.

He found a neat, livable section. A door evidently let to the section that had fallen down. There was a bunk, a small table, and two chairs. The place even had a wooden floor and a stove and fireplace, but no people. He stared all around the small room. There was no place to hide. He stormed around the corner and through the front door. Inside he saw little he hadn't from outside. Near a kerosene lamp with a glass chimney and burning wick, he found a piece of paper. He read the note.

Sorry, O'Grady. We're gone where you'll never find us, unless you can track people in the dark and over slabs of rock. I walked down the canyon a half-mile after we got here just for insurance. Good thing. If you follow us, I'll kill the girl. I've sampled her charms already and she is delicious. Stay back or she's dead!

O'Grady took the note, blew out the lamp, and closed the door on his way out. Where would Loonin go from here? He asked his prisoner the same question when he got back to where he left the horses.

George shook his head. "Honest to God, I don't know of another hiding place up in here anywhere. Been here a year, and there ain't much. Did a lot of prospecting at first."

"You saw them ride off. They had two horses?"

"Yes, the girl rides real good."

"Where could they have gone?"

"A few coyote holes around here, empty mine shafts and tunnels that came up dry."

"Possible." Canyon thought a moment. "We'll go back to the cabin and stay the night. Then in the morning I'll track them, wherever the hell they went."

George rubbed his wrists after O'Grady cut off the rawhide. "You good at tracking?"

"Some have said."

They rode to the cabin and O'Grady lit the lamp, then built a fire in the fireplace and stretched out on the bunk. It had been made of raw lumber of more recent origin than the rest of the cabin. A minute later he went out and brought back his saddlebags and tossed George a sandwich.

"Make it last," O'Grady growled.

An hour later he took a pocketknife from George, and a thin stiletto from his boot, then tied the man's feet together with wet rawhide. By the time it shrank it would have to be cut off his boots in the morning. He tied one of George's wrists to the heavy table leg.

"George, you might be able to get away, but remember, if I hear anything in the dark, I'm shooting first and asking who it is last. You could get real dead that way. Understand? I sleep about as light as a mosquito on a spring breeze. You move much over a few inches, you're taking your life right up there in your good right hand."

"Hell, I'm not going anywhere. Even if I tried I'd probably get lost in the dark. My damn luck."

"See to it," O'Grady growled, and eased toward sleep in the darkness.

Morning came early. O'Grady woke up just before daylight, checked on George, then the horses. They both were in the heavy brush where he had hidden them last night. Back at the cabin he found the tracks of the other horses. Must be the ones that Loonin and Nita used.

Inside he woke up George, gave him a sandwich for breakfast and a long drink of water from the tiny stream. They mounted and O'Grady didn't bother tying George. He looked at the man.

"George, you try to get away and I'll shoot you dead, you understand?"

"Yes, sir, Mr. O'Grady."

"Good, let's ride."

10

Canyon O'Grady and George rode out twenty-five yards from the tumbled-down cabin where they spent the night and then the two men got off their horses and walked, watching the ground closely. They made a circle around the cabin looking for a trail made by two horses. At last they found it, heading almost due north away from the cabin—just the opposite O'Grady would have guessed.

"Where's he going up in there?" George asked. "Nothing I know of in there but dry gullies and washes and desert mountains. Loonin must finally have lost his mind."

"Let's go see."

The trail was easy to follow for the first half-mile, then they came out of the ponderosa along a flinty ridge that dropped away into a deep canyon. The trail skittered along the top of the ridge for a half-mile more, then hit sheet rock and there was not a trace of hoofprints.

The slab of granite was so hard that the shod horses did not make a scratch. The sheet of smooth rock looked endless. O'Grady rode across it along the top of the ridge for a quarter of a mile. There were a dozen places where horses could have gone down now on either side of the ridge. On the left they would have angled back toward the green swatch of ponderosa and water. To the right they would now be in the high desert, where there didn't seem to be a trace of water for dozens of miles.

O'Grady came back from his ride, only this time he dismounted, led his horse, and walked, watching each downslope with close attention. Almost where they came onto the slab of rock, he found the telltale scuffs in the dust and then a clear print.

He walked closer and checked. Loonin had brushed out the shoe prints with a bundle of tree leaves, or perhaps a branch of a pine tree. He ran down the trail and fifty feet down found where the brushing ceased and eight shod hooves took over, leaving a clear trail.

A half-hour later they were down the switchbacks on the steep sides of the canyon and found in the bottom a watercourse where some of the sand was dark with wetness. There had been no attempt by Loonin to dig in for the water that must be below.

The trail continued.

The sun burned down now hotter than usual, since they were in a natural oven, bounded on three sides by heat-reflecting rocks.

"Why in hell is he way out here?" George asked again.

"He knows something we don't," O'Grady said. "Was he a prospector up here before the big strike?"

"Seems to me he said something about that once. Wouldn't catch me prospecting out in here. Say you find some good panning sand. What the hell you gonna wash it with?"

They moved on. The trail was easy to follow. O'Grady could tell that Loonin's pace had picked up. The horses were throwing little puffs of sand away from the front of the shoe.

"Where the hell they going?" George asked again.

"Somewhere where there's water. Their horses, and ours, are going to need some before long."

The trail turned and headed into a smaller canyon. It was less than twenty feet wide and the sides shot up like tall buildings. Soon it looked like a giant V with nothing but sides. A dozen yards more and they had to stop.

"Tracks," O'Grady bellowed. "Dammit, I forgot to watch for tracks. I figured there wasn't anywhere else they could go." He slid off Cormack and walked back the way they had come. He watched the ground, and fifty yards back he stopped and looked at both sides of the ravine.

"They have to be here somewhere," O'Grady growled. "But where in hell?" He moved along the wall, inspecting it foot by foot. He dropped his reins and walked a dozen feet across the small bottom of the gully and began checking the far side.

"Be damned," he said a few minutes later. "George, come over here." Behind some sagebrush that had grown quite high during the rainy season and the occasional cloudburst, there was an opening in the rock barely six feet high and three feet wide—just big enough to lead a horse through.

"A cave," O'Grady said.

"Yeah, a cave, but not just any damn cave. Look above the opening, see that symbol carved in the rock."

O'Grady looked and saw it, a carving that had evidently been done long, long ago, and in detail. It was a winged bird with the body of a man in its talons as it flew skyward.

"This ain't just any cave; it's an Indian burial cave. Most Indians didn't use caves, but the ones around here did, the old, old ones long before the Paiutes settled in this area. Don't know about you, but I ain't setting foot inside there. Stories I heard tell. White men going in and crawling out turned into giant rats."

"Did Loonin know those stories?"

"Damn right! He told me."

"They don't seem to bother him. Look at the tracks of two shod horses going in the doorway. Hell, if he can go in, I'm going in."

"Leave me alone out here?" George said. "Dammit, all right, I'll come, but I warned you."

They led their horses in the black hole and saw that a shaft of light came through some fissure above the cavern was more than twenty feet high and gained in height as they moved inside.

At once it was cool, almost chill compared to the near-hundred-degree heat outside.

Ahead somewhere they could hear water running, splashing and bouncing down a rocky streambed. Twenty feet ahead they found the stream. It came down the side of the floor of the cavern, formed a small pool six feet across, then plunged down a two-foot waterfall and vanished into the ground.

"Damn underground river," George said.

A dozen feet farther on stood the two horses they had been following. Their reins were tied to twenty-pound rocks.

Cormack moved toward the water. If the horse would drink the water, it was probably safe.

"Let's try the water," O'Grady said. "I could use a drink. You bring a canteen?"

"Hell, no."

Both horses drank, then the two men did as well. The water tasted sweet and pure.

They had been quiet as soon as they went inside, and now O'Grady lifted the sawed-off shotgun. He had it tied around his neck by a cord. He cocked the hammers on both barrels and dropped the reins to his horse. He tied them around a rock and then moved forward. He sensed more than heard George close behind him.

It felt like they were in a huge building. Light came in at various points through fissures in the ceiling. O'Grady found at least one spot where a man could crawl out one of the light shafts if the entrance was ever blocked.

There was light enough to see, but he couldn't follow the footprints anymore. Soon a second cavern branched off to the left and then one to the right. They explored each one only to find them dead-end after fifty feet. Back in the main cavern, they moved forward slowly, cautiously.

There was a section a hundred feet long that had no light shafts at all, and it became dusky dark. They walked slowly so they wouldn't drop into a pit.

Then the next light pierced the gloom and they saw what could only be burial mounds. They were perfectly formed square mounds held up by rocks that had been cut and placed one on top of another with no mortar to form an eight-foot square. They rose precisely four feet high, and on top lay a few ancient tools and pottery and a scrap of cloth and bits of leather and obsidian.

They counted twelve of the mounds.

"Maybe a chiefs' burial chamber," O'Grady whispered to George, who backed away from one only to bump into another.

They walked on through and soon found what could have been living quarters. The main cavern had dozens of small offshoots now, and most seemed to have a fire ring and a place that could have been used for sleeping. Stone seats had been cut away in spots, and farther on, what looked like a central council fire ring had been built.

It had been nearing midday when they entered the cave and now a direct shaft of sunlight blazed through an opening directly over the council fire ring and sparkled and shone off it.

"Those rocks, they look like pure gold," George whispered.

The men walked over and checked them. George tried to pick up one but couldn't. It was either mortared in place or tremendously heavy.

Before they could move again, a rifle snarled, sounding like an artillery piece in the confined area of the cave even with the high ceiling.

O'Grady felt something nick his sleeve and he dived behind the fire-ring rocks. "Give it up, Loonin. There's no way out of here except past me. You're trapped."

A voice came from ahead in the cavern.

"Not me, O'Grady. I've got insurance, a train ticket called Nita Gathers. You make one move and she's a corpse. I hear anything from you, you're the next dead man. I've been hunting for this cavern for three years. Now, when I find it, I've got company. Stand up, George and come down here. O'Grady won't hurt you. Come on, I can use you in my new operation. You realize those rocks you're behind are cut from a wall of solid gold?"

"No shit?" George said. He stood up and looked at O'Grady, who shrugged. George took two steps forward toward the voice when the rifle snarled. George bellowed in terror, then pain. He staggered a step backward and the rifle fired again. The second round caught him in the chest and he slammed backward over the gold rocks and died as he fell.

"Nice move, Loonin. Now I can prove murder against you. Gives me every right to shoot your head off."

"Not while I've got my insurance lady. I've got what I want, two saddlebags full of those gold rocks. Now all I have to do is ride back out of here and kill you when you try to come out. I leave Nita here in the desert without a horse and ride back to Virginia City and sell my gold."

"A couple of problems, Loonin. First, I'm never going to let you ride past me. Second, I'll shoot both your horses. Then if you do kill Nita, your insurance policy is no good and I can take my time blasting you into hell."

Loonin laughed. "Yeah, good plan, but it won't work. You're going to be too damn busy." Loonin fired again, then twice more with his rifle. He wasn't shooting at O'Grady, the agent decided. He looked behind him. A natural shelf ran along the side of the cavern, and just behind the gold rock circle a rock wall had been built cutting off part of the shelf into a six-foot-wide room. The bullets churned into a key rock in the face of the stacked-up rock wall and soon it sagged, then fell forward, scattering twenty-pound rocks onto the cavern floor; one or two rolled almost to the fire ring where O'Grady lay.

When the sound of the echoing shots died out, Loonin laughed.

"Yeah, that should do it. Enjoy yourself, Canyon O'Grady. Your new little friends down there want to talk to you."

O'Grady looked behind him. A roiling, rolling mass toppled out of the rock room and fell to the floor. Slowly it surged and vibrated and then rolled forward. Squirming, writhing pieces fell off and slithered away.

Soon the mass would be almost on top of him. O'Grady jumped up and ran. Behind him was the biggest ball of rattlesnakes he had ever seen. There had to be five hundred rattlers there. They had been hibernating, but now that had been shocked from their sleep, they were hungry and furious that their normal cycle had been interrupted.

As O'Grady ran, the rifle spoke again, then twice more, but he ran a zigzag course forward, away from the snakes and deeper into the canyon. He found a niche in the side of the canyon out of sight of the gunman and far enough away from the snakes to be safe.

"Nice try, diamondback, but I'm not snake-bit yet. Now you're next on my list."

"I'll kill the girl, O'Grady. You know I will."

"Hell, who cares? It's your dead body I want. What I should make you do is run barefoot back down the cavern through those rattlers."

There was no response.

"Loonin!" O'Grady drew his six-gun and lunged away from the wall and sprinted for the wall on the other side of the cavern ten yards away. He got there without drawing fire.

Twice more he made the move, then heard something ahead.

"O'Grady! Over here." It was Nita.

"Are you alone?"

"Yes, he ran off into the darkness. Hurry. I'm terrified."

By the time she finished talking, O'Grady was beside her. She threw her arms around him and hugged him tightly.

"Where did he go?"

"That way, straight back. He must know another way out."

They moved forward, hand in hand, O'Grady holding the six-gun. There were shafts of light now and they knew they were moving up an incline. Fifty yards more and they came to a large opening and saw that they were less than twenty feet from the top of the mountain. A rough trail worked up the side.

They paused in a protected place and then O'Grady ran out a few feet on the path and shouted, then hurried back to the cover.

Above, Loonin lifted up and fired his six-gun twice down the path he thought was occupied.

O'Grady had sighted in about where he expected the gunman. When Loonin appeared, O'Grady fired as well and his second round brought a scream of pain from Loonin, who jolted away from the top of the rock wall.

"You hit him," Nita said.

"I hope so. Now all we have to do is go up there and see."

11

O'Grady left Nita in a safe niche in the rock wall and charged up the twenty feet to the rim of the cavern outlet. He made it without being fired at. Over the rim he peered down. It was a gentle slope of a typical Nevada desert mountain, mostly rocks, a few small sagebrush plants, and a lot of sand and thin dirt.

Fifty yards down the slope he saw Loonin. The man limped from the shot in his leg and carried the cast on his right arm stiffly. He was out of range.

O'Grady turned to the girl in the top of the cave. "He's heading for the cavern entrance. I can't let him get there first and kill our horses. Stay right there. I'll be back as soon as I can."

"No," Nita shouted. The girl ran up the steps of rock to the top of the cave and jumped over beside him. "I'm going with you. I can run for miles."

They started down the gentle slope at a run.

"Most of the canyon walls are too steep to climb," O'Grady said. "We'll have to go well down to get into the little gorge."

Nita kept up with him. She grabbed her long skirts and pulled them up almost to her knees, then she could race along beside him. She glanced over. "It might not be ladylike, but right now, I don't care."

O'Grady grinned. "I'll never complain when I can look at a beautiful lady's legs."

A few yards farther on they stopped.

"Loonin came this way, but I'd say he's making a mistake. We need to go more to the south to find a place on that steep wall where we can climb down into the gorge. Let's angle more that direction. The slope is easier as well."

A half-hour later they found the gorge and a place where they could scramble down the sides of the gully. Nita tripped once and fell hard against O'Grady. His hands came up and one caught her firmly, holding one of her breasts. When she had her balance, she looked at him and he moved his hand.

"Sorry, that was the only spot I could catch you," O'Grady said.

She smiled. "No harm done. Fact is, I kind of liked it, but a lady would never admit that." She laughed and they hurried up the small canyon.

O'Grady stopped and looked at the dirt. He found two sets of horseprints but no boot tracks in the dust.

"He hasn't come this way yet, which means we should be ahead of him." They hurried then and made it to the opening. They ran through the entrance so they wouldn't be an easy target in case Loonin was inside. No shots sounded. They found all four horses and led them outside.

They were ready to mount when a pistol shot sounded twenty feet ahead of them near a boulder. The round missed them.

"Down behind the horses," O'Grady yelled. He pulled up the shotgun, pushed back his duster, and leaned around one of the horses. When he saw the edge of a face show around the boulder, he fired the shotgun.

The sawed-off barrel let the birdshot scatter almost at once, and a wailing scream echoed down the canyon after the sound of the shotgun had faded.

"Bastard," the voice boomed. "For that you both die." A six-gun aimed around the boulder and fired four times. One of the horses screamed as it was hit in the side. It surged down the gully past where Loonin hid.

O'Grady motioned to Nita to stay where she was behind Cormack, then he broke open the shotgun and shoved in a new round so both barrels were ready. He cocked the triggers and pushed one of the horses ahead of him as he held on to the saddle. The horse would hide him as he bent low behind it and they both ran for the rock that concealed Loonin.

Loonin's six-gun fired once more and then O'Grady was past the rock. The shotgun boomed twice. O'Grady leveled it under the horse's neck. Loonin took both loads of buckshot in the chest and face from eight feet away.

O'Grady let the horse go and moved toward Loonin. Most of his face was blown away. His chest was a mass of bloody pulp and chopped-up shirt. He had died instantly.

Nita mounted one of the horses and led Cormack up to O'Grady. She looked at the body, then away quickly. "Let's get away from here, O'Grady."

He mounted, caught the reins of the other two horses, and led them out of the canyon.

A half-hour later they had climbed up the switchbacks of the trail they came down on and were back at the sheet rock. They paused a minute to look over the desert mountains.

"Sometimes I think they are so ugly and cruel that they become beautiful," Nita said. "Then other times I wish they were all covered with fir and pine trees."

O'Grady opened the saddlebags on one of the horses that now trailed Cormack on a lead line. The chunks of rock in the bag were heavy. Was it possible that they were almost pure gold and that they had been cut out of a wall of the same metal? If so, it could set off a whole new gold rush. He pushed the rock back in the saddlebag.

Nita had watched him. "What do you think? Loonin went crazy when he found the gold rocks. He was sure they are ninety-nine percent gold."

"We'll let the assayer figure it out. Whatever it is, it's all yours. I'm not sure that I'd want to go digging around in an ancient Indian burial cavern, though. Would you?"

"Not with all those snakes in there. I saw them. There must have been thousands."

O'Grady dug out the remaining sandwiches from his saddlebags. They were mashed and squashed, but they were still good. They each ate one as they walked their mounts back down the way they had come up. An hour later they were at the start of the ponderosa and then soon came to the cabin.

Both had a long drink at the tiny stream.

"What time is it?" Nita asked.

O'Grady hadn't brought his fancy pocket watch. He looked at the sky. "An hour to sundown."

"Good! Let's stay here tonight and go back to town tomorrow."

O'Grady looked at her. "Stay here, all night?"

"Yes, I'm tired." She grinned. "Besides, I thought that maybe you would kiss me again."

"Did Loonin hurt you?"

"No. He wanted to, but I told him I'd find a knife, and when he went to sleep, I'd kill him if he even touched me. He didn't."

She moved toward him and reached up and kissed his lips. Hers were hot and wanting, and when she at last pulled away, she stared hard at him. "Canyon O'Grady, I was hoping you'd want to kiss me again, say ten or fifteen times." She watched him. At last she took his hand and placed it on one of her breasts. "Canyon O'Grady, just how plain do you want me to make it for you?" She caught his hand and pulled him toward the cabin.

At the door he stopped her. "Nita, are you sure?"

In reply she lifted up and kissed him, pushed her breasts against his chest, and with one hand worked between their bodies and rubbed at his crotch. When the long kiss ended, she left her hand on his crotch and looked up at him.

"Mr. O'Grady, I'm so sure that I'm about ready to attack you. Is that sure enough?"

"Plenty. Let me water the horses and picket them, then I'll get some wood for a fire and come in. We should have one more sandwich left in the saddle-bags."

Nita watched him her eyes bright. "Hurry," she said, and pushed open the cabin door and looked inside.

Ten minutes later they sat on the bunk with the one blanket from Nita's saddle that Loonin had provided for her. They had lit the lamp and started a small fire in the fireplace.

"You know there's not another person within five miles of us right now," Nita said. "I like that. It makes me feel all safe and secure." She unbuttoned six of the fasteners down the front of her dress.

He kissed her hands, then the slice of her creamy white chest that showed below her neck.

"How does it make you feel, Canyon O'Grady?"

"Warm and secure, and wanting to help you with those buttons."

"Good." Nita moved her hands and let him open the fasteners. She reached up and kissed him on the cheek, then on the lips, and his tongue probed against her lips.

"Oh, my, yes. That feels so nice, so good, so right."

He reached in past her open dress top and pushed his hand around one of her breasts.

"Yes, darling Canyon, I love that!"

He petted her breast, caressed it, then moved his hand to the other orb. She gasped and clung to him for a moment. He took out his hand and undid the rest of the buttons and pushed the dress top off her shoulders. It fell to her waist. Only a thin shift covered her. He lifted it over her head and she looked down at her bare breasts, then at him.

"Are they . . . are they all right?"

"Beautiful." He bent and kissed one, and she shuddered. He kissed it again and she humped her hips at him, then he pulled half of her breast into his mouth and chewed on it gently.

Nita fell back on the bunk, her eyes closed tightly, her face distorted as she gasped. Her whole body shook and vibrated as a spasm shot through her again and again. She whimpered and pulled him toward him until he lay partly on top of her.

At last she opened her eyes. "Oh, Canyon! Oh, Canyon, so wonderful. Please kiss me again."

He kissed her lips, leaning over her, crushing her breasts as he lay against her. She worked her hand down to his crotch and found his hardness and rubbed it as long as the kiss lasted.

He sat up and she undid his belt and then the buttons on his fly and looked at him. He nodded. She reached inside and pushed back short underwear and tugged his stiff penis out of his pants. She stroked him, then moved over so he could lie beside her on the bunk. She took his hand and put it on one of her legs. He worked gently upward and under her skirt. He touched her bare flesh and she gave a little cry, but when he looked at her, she was smiling.

His hand worked higher and higher and she pulled his lips down to hers.

"Kiss me when you touch it," she said, then kissed him with such force that he forgot for a minute what he was doing with his hand. He moved higher, felt the pubic hair and then the wetness, and he brushed his fingers over her treasure.

Nita sighed and broke off the kiss.

"Yes, darling Canyon, it's all right. Please let's do it right now before we take off all our clothes. Can you? Right now!" She spread her legs and lifted her skirt to show her naked and open heartland.

"Now? This way?"

"Yes. I'll tell you why. Please, darling Canyon . . . right now!"

He lifted up and moved over her leg until he was between her white thighs. Her skirts covered her breasts and she nodded at him. Slowly her knees lifted and he went down and touched her wetness, then probed with his lance and slid in an inch. He stopped.

"Please, more, all the way. Right now."

He eased forward and found her lubricated, so he drove in hard and deep until they hit bone to bone. She sighed and kissed his chin, tears glistening in her eyes.

She climaxed again; a long low wail escaped from her lips as her small hips pounded up against his and her body shook and rattled with six roaring climaxes before she eased off and touched sweat on her forehead.

"Oh, glory, you do have a way with a girl." She squeezed him with her inside muscles. "I bet it's almost your turn."

Her long blond hair bunched behind her head now and framed her pretty face. Her soft blue eyes were laughing at him. "You probably thought I was a virgin, didn't you?"

"Matter of fact, I did."

"You know that some girls like sex as much as boys do?"

"I've heard." He began to stroke into her and she caught his rhythm and ground her round little bottom in a circle against him, first one way, then the other. Her inside muscles gripped and released him on every stroke, and the combination rushed O'Grady toward a climax like a teenager's. He couldn't hold it off.

A few seconds later he exploded, bursting into her with a hard drive and then eight more as he planted his seed.

12

The next morning they rode into Virginia City without being noticed, which was fine with O'Grady. They stopped behind the mining-equipment store and Nita ran inside. O'Grady found a sturdy wooden packing box behind the store and took out all of the gold rocks and put them in the box. The four saddlebags of rocks almost filled the box.

By the time O'Grady had the job done, Gathers came running out. "Thank God you found her, O'Grady. I owe you more than I can tell you. Nita says the first night she threatened the kidnappers and they let her alone, and then last night she said you were a perfect gentleman. I want to thank you again." He looked at the box. "What's in there?"

"Not sure yet." O'Grady opened the lid and took out one of the smallest chunks, about three inches long. "You were a prospector. What do you think it is?" He handed the rock to Gathers.

The merchant frowned at the sight of it and almost dropped it. "My God! It's so heavy. But it can't be." Gathers' eyes went wide and his face exploded with a wild grin. "O'Grady, I looked for ten years for something like this. That's about the purest form of gold nugget I've ever seen. It must be ninety-five percent pure gold!"

O'Grady took the chunk and with his pocketknife

shaved six or seven slivers off it, each about an eighth of an inch thick. He put the chunk back in the box and closed the lid. "Mr. Gathers, sir. Here is about a hundred pounds of the stuff. If it's as good as you think, it should be worth somewhere around thirty thousand dollars. Now it belongs to Nita. Pay her back for her pain and suffering during the kidnapping."

"Hey, O'Grady, dammit! Don't just stand there. I've got to know. How did you get it? Where does it come from? I want to get out there and stake a claim!"

"Doubtful. This country has enough problems with the silver. Anyway, I'm not sure I could find the same spot again. I think Loonin knew something about it. Then I chased him and he found the right little canyon way up there in those desert mountains. He might just have stumbled into it looking for a place to hide."

"My God, O'Grady. Didn't you make a map on your way out? We've got to go back in there this afternoon so you don't forget where it is. If there's a lot of it, it could be worth millions and millions of dollars."

"I don't think so, Gathers. It's too easy. Gold should come hard, the way silver does. Dig it out a mile underground. Besides, do you like rattlesnakes?"

"Hell no. Hate the things."

"Last time I saw the gold there were at least five hundred rattlesnakes waking up, crawling all over it. A hibernation ball of snakes eight feet thick. Maybe they protect the gold, I'm not sure."

"Snakes I can deal with for gold ore like this. I bet Nita can lead me back there. Oh, no, damn! She's worse than I am about directions. She'd get lost going around the block. Did you ride north or south out of here?"

"North, I guess. You see, I'm a stranger in this country."

Gathers laughed without any mirth. "You're not going to tell me, are you? A real bonanza, a mother lode, and you won't tell me where it is."

"Gathers, no amount of gold is worth getting killed for. None of us should have made it alive out of there. Remember, two men died getting this much out. I'm not going back, and I don't think Nita will either. I'm making up for it, though. This box should be worth that thirty thousand dollars we mentioned. I'll get these shavings assayed, then you can sell the chunks a few at a time so nobody gets wise. I'd guess you should smash or crumble up those chunks. Too obvious this way."

Gathers scratched his head. "I just don't understand. You know where there's a mountain of this stuff and you won't go back after it. Won't even tell me where to look?"

"About the size of it. I'm a federal employee, not a prospector. Nothing that I do in the course of my work for the government can enrich me in any way. I find a five-dollar gold piece, I turn it in. I pick up a suitcase full of money, I turn it in. You're just lucky I'm not turning in this box of yellow rocks here. You want to do something with them, that's fine with me. Right now I forgot I even had them."

Gathers stared at O'Grady. "Son, you're a sick man. You must be out of your mind. Who in hell could forget about something like this? We'll go home, fix you a good supper, and you can have a drink or two, then you'll feel better and we can sit down and draw a map, just the way you remember it."

O'Grady shook his head. "I'm fine, and a meal and some drinks won't change my mind. The place was spooky, eerie. I'm not going back." He pointed at the wooden box. "I suggest you pile some merchandise on top of this box, unless you want to move it inside."

"Yes, yes, right now, I want it all inside. Give me a hand."

Together they lifted the surprisingly heavy box and carried it through the back door and to the small office. They put it on the floor and pushed it under the desk.

O'Grady stood up. "Now, as for me, I need to take these rock scrapings and see if I can get them assayed through a third party."

U.S. Marshal Ben Jones stared at the shavings of gold in O'Grady's clean handkerchief.

"I'm no expert, but that looks damn near like pure gold. I'll get it assayed for you in confidence."

"One other small matter: one man, name not known except for George, and one Rush Loonin have ceased to exist. Loonin shot George, and in the course of our chase, my shotgun helped Loonin on his way to hell. Bodies not recoverable."

"Did I hear something about a kidnapping?" Jones asked.

"Indeed. The Gathers girl. Loonin took her and was trying to kill me and get my horse. He failed on all three counts."

"You think Loonin killed the mine inspector for Moudry?"

"Probably, Marshal, but we can't prove it. I killed Loonin in self-defense and to save Miss Gathers. I'll write a report for you."

"I should get more details about location," the marshal said.

"No. Let it lay. The report will cover you."

"What about the gold?"

"A chance happening."

"Have you heard about the legend of the lost Indian burial cavern with its wall of gold?"

"Can't say that I've heard that wild story, Marshal. Is it to be believed?"

"The legend said the wall of gold was almost pure, a wall of pure gold ten times the height of a man. Just like those shavings in your handkerchief."

"Now, don't that beat all, Marshal. But I don't have time to chase legends. I have to work on our friend Moudry. If he's guilty of the murder of Luke Denker, it's my job to prove it and charge him in a court of law."

"Indeed it is, Mr. O'Grady." Jones stood. "Now, let me take those gold shavings over to the assayer's office. It's in one corner of the bank. Smart man that banker. Assays it and buys it all in one operation. Looks like about two ounces here, over forty dollars' worth. Shall I sell it after it's assayed?"

"Yes, and put the cash in your coffee fund, or put it in the poor box or the church collection. All I want is a written assay report."

The men left the marshal's office and went separate ways. O'Grady walked down to D Street and up the steps to Julia's house of ill repute. Time for another reading on the community and any extra activity up at the Bonanza. Julia would know.

Just inside the door he stepped into the parlor, which was as garish as before. The same man with the derby hat and red suspenders tinkled away on the upright piano.

A girl glided up to him and held out her hand. "Good evening, sir, I'm Billie Jo. I'd be more than glad to show you around upstairs, unless you're here to see someone in particular."

"Miss Cosette is the one I want to see on some personal business. Is she in?"

"It's a little early for her, but I'll go see." She hesitated. "My, but you are a fine one. When you're done with your business, why not stop by and see me? I give total satisfaction." She ran the tip of her pink tongue around her open mouth.

"I bet you do, but I'm a little on the busy side this afternoon."

Julia Cosette was up and dressed. She put on her makeup as he watched.

"Making any progress on the Denker murder?" she asked as soon as he walked in.

"Some. Hoping you could help me."

"Be glad to, drop your pants." Julia paused a beat, then bellowed in laughter. "Usually that gets me a laugh." She sobered. "So, how can I help?"

"Moudry, he ever come to see your ladies?"

"Hell, no! He's got his own private whore. She used to work for me. He bought her off and she's just servicing him now."

"Damn, I was hoping he talked in his sleep or at least when he was in heat."

"He didn't, but one of his men has a loose mouth. Who was it telling me? Lila, I think." She went to the door and called. A minute later a tall black girl came in. She was slender and willowy with modest breasts and a beautiful face.

"Lila, didn't one of your customers say something was stewing up at the Bonanza? Some big deal coming?"

Lila looked at O'Grady and grinned. "Honey, you want to know about that? You come into my bed and I'll tell you exactly what he said."

"No time for that right now, Lila. The man is a friend and in a hurry. What did the whacker say?"

"He's a guard for Moudry, pretty high up, I'd think. Said he wouldn't be in next Thursday as usual because he's got to go on a special little work detail. He said it seemed damned strange stealing from yourself, but that was exactly what Moudry was going to do. Usually this gent brings me a present. Said he couldn't this time, lost most of his cash at a poker game, but he would next time. I asked him if it was payday, and he said, Oh, yeah, monthly payday, and he was going to help bring in the payroll from Carson City.''

Julia let one breast pop out of her gown and looked at O'Grady, but he was watching Lila.

"He was bringing in the payroll and then he said something about stealing from yourself," O'Grady said. "What did he mean by that?"

Lila shrugged and let one breast come out of her robe. "I don't know, honey, but I sure would like to talk it over with you for about an hour."

"Sorry, Lila." O'Grady took no special notice of the breast displays. His brow wrinkled and he walked around the room. "Stealing from himself? Would Moudry steal his own payroll? Why? Wells Fargo isn't insuring it, they don't even come in here. What good would it do him?"

"Might be some help," Julia said, covering herself. "About six months ago the big miners got together. They were bringing in their payrolls separately from the bank in Carson City. Five or six times a gang jumped them, held them up, and got away with the cash. They wanted a better system. Now they all bring in their payroll cash together in one coach armed with a half-dozen men inside and three in front and three in back. Hasn't been a robbery of the payroll since they all got in one pot, so as to speak."

"Now it makes sense," O'Grady said. He stood behind the sleek black girl where she sat on a chair. His hands went to her shoulders and he gently massaged her shoulders and neck muscles.

"Hey, that feels wonderful," Lila said.

"The four of them have their payroll on the rig. If one of the four mine-owners robs the coach, he doesn't lose any money and profits from the payroll of the other three. Since he evidently 'lost' money too, he wouldn't be a suspect."

"Sounds damn sneaky to me," Lila said. She caught O'Grady's hands and pulled them forward and down to her bare breasts. "I need some massaging down here too, honey," she said.

O'Grady caressed them a moment, pinched the dark nipples, and then patted her shoulder.

"Sorry to pet and run, but I've got a man to talk to. Ladies, you've been most helpful. We just might have an angle on getting Mr. Moudry to pay his dues in the game of murder." He walked to the door.

"You come back and see Lila, nice man," she said. "I'll take a short vacation from work and do you for free."

"Best offer I've had today," O'Grady said. He waved at them both and hurried out the door and up the hill to C Street. He hoped that the saddle-maker was open for business.

As he walked down C Street, he saw four new stores being constructed. Saw lumber had been hauled in from Carson City, he guessed. One store was almost ready, another in the framing stage, and on a third, workmen had just begun construction on a second floor. In two years there would be ten times this many business firms in town if the silver boom continued.

The town was taking on a permanent status not seen in the gold-rush placer-mining areas. There a tent town went up overnight, then a few frame buildings. But all too often the placer gold was worked out in six months or a year, sometimes two years. If the mother lode wasn't found, the gold would be soon gone and so would the miners—and the town.

O'Grady pushed open the wood-framed screen door. When it closed, it hit a small lever that triggered a mechanical set of chimes. O'Grady hadn't noticed it the last time he was there.

"Good morning, Orrin. How good are you on voice identification this afternoon?"

"Damn good," Orrin said, and laughed. "That's usually a stall so I get you to say something more, but for you I don't need it, Canyon O'Grady. You've got just a slight little Irish lilt left in your King's English."

"I'm back to work, Orrin. I'm looking for some background. They used to have trouble with mine payrolls getting stolen coming into town. What did they do about it?"

"The four big miners didn't trust the brand-new local bank. They formed a cooperative and all brought their payrolls in together with twice as many guards as any one mine had been using. Haven't had a robbery since. Why?"

"Just wondering. I might rob the payroll."

"You might fart in Washington, D.C., too, if you eat enough beans."

O'Grady grinned. "Hey, Orrin, I'm laughing. I'm just not making any noise."

"Blind humorists have trouble with that. At least I don't pry too hard. I hear your buddy Rush Loonin is dead."

"True."

"How?"

"Got himself shot up north a ways."

Orrin went back to work on a piece of leather he was cutting. He checked the outline he had scratched in the leather, matched it against a piece he was duplicating. Then he began working with the razor-sharp knife.

"You ever hear of a legend about an ancient Indian burial ground around here?" O'Grady asked.

"Heard it, don't believe it."

"Good, I don't have to cut you in for half."

"I'd just get lost in the mountains anyway. I never was any good in my first job as a professional tracker and scout." There was a short silence. "You better be grinning, cowboy, or I'm going to stitch razors just under the surface of your saddle so they'll work up and cut your ass proper."

"I'm grinning, I'm grinning."

They talked for another hour before O'Grady offered to buy Orrin supper. The invitation was accepted at once.

13

Orrin insisted that they eat at the Beanery. It was close by and he said he liked the way Elly Handshoe cooked.

"Seems more like down-home cooking to me than one of them more fancy places. I'm just common folks."

O'Grady gave in and the blind man walked with his hand on O'Grady's arm as they went the half-block down the boardwalk and into Elly's eatery.

She grinned at them from behind the small counter. "Oh, damn we got troubles now, folks. I got this wild redhead and a blind man walking into my place. I don't know whether to get my gun or my flyswatter." She waved at O'Grady and touched Orrin's shoulder and then bent in slowly and kissed his cheek.

Orrin laughed. "Talk about beautiful. This is the most beautiful woman I've ever seen."

"Orrin, you been stone-blind since you was a baby," Elly said. "You ain't never seen a woman." She roared with generous laughter, her whole body shaking.

"You don't miss a trick, do you, Elly?" He guffawed and she punched him in the shoulder. He went down the counter to a table next to the small windows along the front, found it vacant, and sat down. O'Grady sat across from him.

"I'd guess you're planted at my table," Orrin said.

"About as planted as I want to be for a good number of years," O'Grady said.

They had just finished their dinner—roast beef, a slab an inch thick and smothered with horseradish sauce—when a man burst in the front door. He was tall and slender, with blue clay stuck to his boots and his heavy pants. His face was glowing, and as soon as he got inside the door, he screamed.

"Elly Handshoe, you're a rich woman. You never have to wash another pot or cook another thing in your life."

The man ran toward the counter and Elly came out with a small frying pan she held by the handle like a club.

"Sandforth Handshoe, have you lost your mind, or are you stinking drunk for the first time in your life?" she shrilled.

"Both and all three, Elly!" He grabbed her, frying pan and all, and swung her around in a circle and then did a fancy jig. "Remember them two ten-foot chunks of claim we had side by side up on Gold Hill? It just came in. Not down twenty feet when they hit a vein near to a foot across and it's heading straight down. The boys figure it should be worth at least forty thousand dollars the first week. We're rich, Elly. We're stinking rich!"

Elly slowly lowered the pan and then dropped it on the counter. Then she lifted her long skirts and did a fancy jig of her own. She stopped and watched the half-dozen diners. "Tell anyone who comes in that I'm rich and don't cook no more. Anybody who wants to can serve up a plate or two of food. Just clean up any mess you make." Elly patted her short brown hair in place and looked at her husband. "Mr. Handshoe, would you care to show the mistress of the rich silver mine the way up the slope so I can see just how stinking rich I am before it gets dark?''

"It would be my pleasure, Mrs. Handshoe. Right this way.''

As they walked through the front door, everyone inside applauded.

"Couldn't have happened to a nicer couple,'' Orrin said. He stood with O'Grady, who dropped a paper dollar on the counter near the change drawer as they walked outside.

O'Grady walked Orrin back to his leather shop, then went up the hill with what seemed to be half the town to look at the latest big strike.

The claim was near the top and on the close side, but didn't look like much. Neither did the Ophir from the surface. A knot of thirty men stood around the shaft, which had been sunk into the ground for about twenty feet. A windlass to wind up the buckets of soil and ore groaned as it brought up a full container. Now they were coming loaded with ore, rich blue rock silver ore.

Elly stood there like a queen pointing to her coyote hole and explaining how much money they were going to make.

"Hell, in a couple of months we'll have money to burn,'' Sandforth shouted.

Somebody in the crowd laughed. "Hell, Sandy, we'll expect you to buy a round for the house whenever you come in a saloon,'' the man said.

"Damned if I won't—next week when I can afford it.''

O'Grady knew the men would hold him to his promise. After all, money was for spending. Sandforth would probably buy the house a round and then a dozen before he was through.

The coyote hole the two men worked in was about

six feet wide. There were no boards on the sides to shore it up in case of unstable dirt. The men just trusted to the solid nature of the rocky soil and clay they were digging through.

O'Grady got a look at the vein. It was blue, all right, and positioned to the left side of the hole but almost in the middle of the twenty feet of the claim. The rest of the claim was not being worked.

"Heading straight down, but wherever that vein goes, it's our vein," Sandforth told the man. "The practice around here is that the man who cuts into a vein owns it, even if it runs underground into somebody else's claim. We're rich, we're stinking rich. We've got money to burn."

"Hey, Sandy. Light my cigar with a ten-dollar bill, would you?"

"Next week, friend," Sandforth said with a gleam in his eye.

O'Grady walked back down the hill. He still moved with caution: never going around the corner of a building close to the wood, never rushing into a store or a building without looking it over and trying to see who was inside. On the street he checked both ways, watching for anyone loitering and perhaps waiting for him. Such caution had kept him alive more than once when he could have been killed.

Loonin was gone, but he was sure that Moudry would send someone else after him. He just didn't know who or where. Until the gunner showed up, he had to keep doing his job. How else could he pin the killing on Moudry? The key witness, the killer himself, was gone. Who now? What now?

Lila. She was his best contact. He walked down to D Street and up the steps to Julia's whorehouse. Lila sat in the parlor. Her hair was arranged all fancy on top of her head, and the gown she wore showed off half of each breast. She came over to him at once.

"Couldn't stand not seeing the rest of Lila, right, redheaded man?"

"Partly. Where can we talk?"

"Upstairs. We can talk and play all we want."

"Let's go."

The room was small, but much larger than some he had seen in similar situations. The bed looked soft and had a clean spread over it. There were two armchairs and a dresser and two pictures on the wall. One of an older version of Lila with a baby in each arm. It was a tintype. The other tintype was smaller of a young black boy.

"Where is your son?" he asked.

Lila looked up quickly. She had been unsnapping the front of her dress and now lowered it to her waist, her hand-size breasts popping out firm and erect.

"Jason's his name, he's with my mamma in Chicago." She stared at O' Grady, big brown eyes wide with a new appreciation. "Nobody never asked about him before."

"Lila, tell me about the man you talked to about that payroll thing. Does he have a name?"

"Yeah, but I tell you, he'll kill me, sure as sassafras. I know him. He's a mean bastard."

"I won't let him hurt you."

"O'Grady, you're a nice man, but you can't live in this room twenty-four hours a day with me. He could come anytime."

"Not if he's in jail, or in a grave."

She watched him with that curious little tilt of her head that told O'Grady a lot about her anger and her spunk and fight. When she thought it through, she nodded. "All right. I can tell you because he probably

112

talked about it to some others as well. But you be sure to arrest him if you can.''

''Done.''

''His name is Punk and he's a night guard at the ore shed. He's about five feet eight and mean as hell. Likes me to hit him with a stick when he comes in, but he don't hit me.'' She slid out of the fancy-ball dress and wore nothing under it. She was as sleek naked as he had guessed.

Lila sat down beside him on the bed and reached for his crotch. He caught her hand and she looked up surprised.

''Hey, my party.''

''What do you mean, Lila?''

''I'm not giving you this information for free. You got to pay me, cowboy.''

''Just what kind of payment do you expect?''

Lila smiled, a beautiful chocolate smile that was good enough to gobble up by the spoonful. ''Canyon O'Grady, you have a naked woman sitting beside you on a bed with a locked door over there and the lady is reaching for your crotch. Just what kind of payment do you think she wants?''

He let go of her hand and she unbuttoned the first fastener on his fly. ''I just ain't never had me a handsome redhead like you before. Fair is fair.''

She worked on his fly again.

''You sure make it hard, pretty lady, to be true to my wife and family.''

She laughed. ''O'Grady, if you're married, you sure not wearing a wedding band. Handsome man like you ain't married yet. You're footloose and cock-free.''

Her hand snaked inside his clothes and found him.

''Oh, my, yes! Now, you gonna make me rape you right here or just seduce you?''

''Seduction sounds good.''

Lila grinned and began to unbutton his shirt. "Been a long time for me. Seducing, I mean. Once, about three years ago, this kid came in clutching his two dollars. He was so scared he couldn't even spit. I asked him up. It took him a half-hour to get his pants off and by then I saw he'd lost about three loads. But we finally got the job done. Afterward he pulled on his pants and hid his face and ran out the door."

"Promise I won't hide my face."

"Good." She kissed his cheek, then pulled back. "Oh, you don't mind a whore's kiss."

"No such word in my language as 'whore.' I like the term 'lady' lots better."

Lila smiled. "I don't get called that much." She pulled off his shirt, then his boots, and finally his pants.

"You know anything more about this Punk?"

"Nope. Been to see me regular for about three months, every Thursday. Tips me a dollar, which I get to keep. Getting me a nest egg to move back to Chicago."

"Why Chicago?"

"A few freemen there with black skin. I'm needing a husband about now."

"Might not have to go to Chicago. One of the best men I've known, white or black, lives right here."

"Sweet Orrin?"

"The same."

"He's blind."

"Sounds like your heart is blind. He loves you already, don't you know that? He's making a good living. A lady could do far worse. Besides, you'd save all that stage money getting to Chicago."

"Shut up, white man, let me run my own life."

"Just trying to nudge you in the right direction."

She smiled at him. "Thanks. I've thought about it before. He's so sweet and gentle."

"And has a bank account and a fine reputation—"

"Shut up, white man." She rolled on top of his naked body and grinned. "When I seduce a man, I usually drop one of my tits into his mouth. Would that work here?"

"Try it and see."

She eased a large, firm nipple into Canyon's mouth and clutched the sides of his head as he began to tease the dark flesh with his tongue. "Oh, oh, yes." She shuddered when Canyon pulled away and found her other nipple. His tongue flitted across the hardened flesh and Lila cried out again.

She moved her hips and then again to find his maleness. She slid him deep inside her until they were nailed together.

Her black hips danced above him as she knew exactly what to do to excite him. His passion grew and grew until he couldn't control it anymore and he exploded with a great burst into her half a dozen times.

"Not bad for your first time," she said, still in control, still the teacher. He reached between them and before she could protest, he found the small sensitive node. His finger, moistened by her fluids, danced across the hard tissue. Her breath came like a steam engine and her body shook, and then she climaxed with a long wailing call to some primal instinct. Her body spasmed twenty times before she at last sighed a long panting breath and relaxed on top of him.

Ten minutes later she lifted up and came away from him. They both sat on the bed and she glanced at him almost shyly at first, then with an honest smile.

"O'Grady, nobody's pleasured me that way for more than two years. I won't let them. That's something private and not business."

"This wasn't business, it was honest respect. Dammit, Lila, why don't you just go—"

She put her hand over his mouth. "Shut up, white man, let me live my own life." She stood and shrugged into her dress. "Man, you get your pants on, there might be some big stud downstairs who wants some chocolate candy, and he wants to eat me up. Come on now, I'm a working girl and I got to make a living."

"Shut up, black lady," he said softly, and she grinned.

14

Edwin Moudry wiped at his tearing eyes again, then pushed the linen handkerchief away.

The short, overweight man with the broad, plain face stared at the messenger. "You sure it was both of them?"

"Yes, sir. Our man in the marshal's office got it right off the report O'Grady wrote. Loonin shot George Propar for some reason and later O'Grady shot Loonin. The bodies are what he called 'unrecoverable.' "

"Yes, yes, and O'Grady and the girl got away. Goddamn! All right, you told me; now get the hell out of here. I've got enough troubles without looking at you, too."

The man left at once.

Moudry slumped in the big leather chair behind his desk in the office building at the Bonanza Mine. He realized now he didn't have a man who was good with a gun. His guard chief Punk Buolic was his next best man. Punk was no bargain. Damn, he'd have to do.

He sent a man to bring Punk, who came in looking a little sleepy. He was on the night-guard team.

"You just got promoted, Buolic. You're now my security chief. We talked last week about doing a little surprise raid on the payroll shipment from Carson City."

"Yes, Mr. Moudry."

"It's on. The coach will be leaving at the same time. One of the other mine-owners wanted to reduce the guard force to four from eight, and we all went along with him. Four men inside with rifles, and the driver. Where will the best place be to hit them?"

"There's a steep upgrade about ten miles out where the trail goes around a sharp bend," Buolic said. "I've ridden that rig a dozen times. That's the best spot. It almost comes to a stop. We take out the lead horse or the driver and then pick off the guards inside with rifles."

"Fine. I want you to hire two new men to add to our guard force. New men always take the payroll ride down to Carson City and back. They call it easy duty. These two might not come back. I don't want any of your men identified. If they are, you'll kill all the guards."

"Yes, sir."

"Now get out of here and hire those two new guards. Give them regular duty, but tell them you'll leave Thursday to ride to Carson City for the return Friday. That's two nights away. You hit them hard, trash the coach if you want to and then ride on to Carson City and camp down there along the river. You stay there for two days, then bring the payroll back up here to me by one of the back trails. Use a packhorse if you need to."

"What about the other men, sir?"

"Bring them back with you. How many will you need to hit the coach?"

"I'll take six men and me. That should do it. Sir, could I make a suggestion?"

"Is it any good?"

"Yes, sir. I'd rather go to Carson City and pick up six men there, drifters, down-and-outers who can shoot. I pay them fifty dollars for the raid and then they ride on down into California and we'll never see them again."

"And if I don't like that suggestion, Buolic?"

"Then I'll have to kill the six men who help me, so there won't be any witnesses to talk."

"Yes, yes, I see what you mean." Moudry lit a long black cigar and tossed one to Punk, who bit off the end and lit it. "All right, hire the two new guards, put them to work, and assign them to the payroll run. Tell them when to leave Thursday and where to report in Carson City. Then you get down to Carson City. Ride your own horse and leave about three A.M. this coming morning. If anything goes wrong, you'll be looking up from your grave, Buolic."

"Yes, sir, I know."

"Now, the other problem."

"O'Grady?"

"Yeah, Buolic. Between now and tonight when you leave, I want O'Grady dead. There's a two-hundred-dollar bonus for you if you blast the son of a bitch into hell."

"I've got some ideas," Punk said.

"Don't tell me, just do it. Today, tonight. . . . do it."

"Yes, sir. I was thinking—"

"Out! I don't want to know. Get out of here."

Buolic turned and left the room with a small grin. For a moment Moudry wondered if he had misread the man. Would he take off into California with the payroll?

Slowly Moudry shook his head. The man was clever, but not that clever or smart. He knew he would be tracked down and killed. He'd be back with the money.

"Belle," the short man bellowed. The door into her

apartment cracked open and a bare foot and then bare leg slid into sight.

"Belle, dammit get in here, my nerves are all jangled."

The leg drew back and an arm came through, then the flash of a bare breast.

"I'm just getting out of my bath," her small voice said.

"Dammit, Belle, get your cute little ass in here. I'm getting horny as hell just watching parts of you."

She walked through the door naked and posed for him.

"Yeah, that's my girl. Get it over here and see if you can coax me into getting hard."

Punk Buolic left the mine office and hurried down to C Street, where he turned in at the worst little saloon in town. They didn't have any girls or cribs upstairs. They didn't have any fancy games of chance. There were four small tables for drinking or playing cards and a stand-up bar made from big barrels and some sawed planks.

Punk waved at some of the men, talked with the barkeep for a minute, and then went into a back room. It was smaller, had a table and one chair and a bottle of whiskey and one glass. He poured a shot and threw it down.

A minute later the door opened and a man came in.

"Can you shoot?" Punk asked.

"Damn right. Had a rifle when I was ten and had to bring home supper for our family of eight—or we didn't eat. We always ate." The man had a thin scraggly beard, a reddish nose, and eyes that drooped partly closed.

"You drunk?"

"A little. Life seems better that way."

"You shoot good when you're drunk?"

"Better than when I'm sober."

"You ever killed a man?"

"Now and again. No law after me."

"Good. Can you handle a Sharps fifty?"

"Like it's half of my arm."

"You want to earn fifty dollars, today?"

"Yeah, but pay it to the barkeep, Jonesy, or I'll get drunk and give it all away."

"I can do that." Buolic watched the man. He seemed right. Punk waved the man to follow him and they went out the alley door, down to the street, then back to C Street and sat in front of the hardware store in two captain's chairs.

"Man I'm interested in has flame-red hair, he's over six feet tall and he has to die today if possible. Stays at the Big Strike Hotel across the street there. I've seen this guy. I'll point him out to you, and we'll keep him nailed down while you figure out a spot to shoot from."

"Sure as hell help to know what he looks like."

"You will."

It wasn't quite dark when O'Grady left Lila. He was wondering how he could find this man Punk. Couldn't be many men in a place this size by that name. He stopped in at a bar and asked the barkeep if he'd ever heard of a man named Punk in town.

The barman shook his head.

After the third barkeep gave him a negative reaction, O'Grady headed for the Big Strike Hotel. He ambled along the boardwalk across from the hardware store and went up the steps.

Across the street there was a hurried conference and then Punk Buolic rushed down the street to the saw-dust saloon and took the big .50-caliber Sharps out the back door and up the vacant lot next to the hardware store.

"I'll get him out of the hotel. You can stay right here and hit him as he comes down the front steps." Buolic watched the bushwhacker to see that he understood. "This guy might change clothes or something. Have to hurry before it gets dark."

Buolic got a nod from the man, who had slid a round into the single-shot, big .50 and lay down beside the foundation of the store where he was out of sight. Yeah, he could do it.

Punk ran across the street and into the hotel. The clerk looked up. Buolic handed him two one-dollar bills. "Send a note up to Canyon O'Grady's room saying that a miner from the Bonanza wants to talk to him on the front steps of the hotel. Do it right now. And you don't know who left the message, right?"

The clerk looked at him, then down at the two dollars. That was as much as he made in almost two days of work. He nodded.

Five minutes later, Punk Buolic crouched beside his gunman who was lying beside the store's foundation; only the muzzle of the big .50 showed. They waited.

Two men stood on the steps of the hotel. One was a drummer who had just come in off a new stage; he had a display case of knives and pistols. He had registered and was checking the lay of the stores for his visits the next day.

The second man was a miner, drunk enough to know he was lost, but sober enough to know he had to ask somebody where his tent was.

Buolic waited for a man to come out the doors. Five minutes later the right one came out. He had on a low-crowned hat and the same clothes as before.

"It's our man," Buolic said to the gunman. "The

one at the doors in the brown hat and brown vest. Take him out now!''

The pause lengthened out and another man came out of the hotel. O'Grady moved to the left, and just as the second man walked around O'Grady, the gunman fired. The round sped true to its aim, only it hit the wrong man. Both had moved and the man behind O'Grady took the bullet in the chest and slammed backward almost to the hotel door.

O'Grady knew the sound. He sprinted for the cover of a buggy going past the hotel, bent low behind the horses, and ran down the street with them for half a block; then he crossed the street and came back on the side the gunman must have used. He saw the most obvious place, one side or the other of the hardware store directly across from the hotel. Empty lots on both sides of it. He ran down the boardwalk and saw no one on this side of the store.

O'Grady had his six-gun out as he sprinted for the far side of the hardware store. He saw someone with a long gun running down the side of the store for the alley.

O'Grady snapped off a shot, but the man was out of range. He charged down the rocky-soil path as the figure vanished to the right. At the corner, O'Grady bent low and looked around. The man with the rifle stood three feet away, a six-gun up and aimed chest-high. O'Grady fired upward at the man, hit him in the shoulder; he spun away, firing twice at the slice of face, but missed. Before the bushwhacker's second shot got off, O'Grady had fired again himself, the round striking the gunman in the chest and stilling his heart as he slammed against the end of the store and slumped into the dirt.

O'Grady looked at the long gun, a Sharps, that had been set against the hardware store's back wall. That was the gun that had been fired. He looked around in the alley, but could see no one else. He had the man who had tried to kill him, but the question now couldn't be answered about who had hired him to do the job.

O'Grady waited for Marshal Jones to come, told him the story, and was backed up by the drummer, who had been on the steps and had seen the flash and smoke of the weapon across the street.

"Not much help to you, I'm afraid," Ben Jones said. "I'll need the usual statement to close this out. I just hope the dead man has some papers on himself to identify who he was."

"That would be a help. But like you say, it's no benefit for my main problem. You find out about that assay?"

"Yep. Like you figured, it assayed out ninety-four percent pure. Good as gold. He asked me where it came from, but I said I had no idea, which I don't. I sold it to him and put the money in my relief fund."

"Good, now forget about it."

"Hard thing to do in a mining town. But I'll try."

O'Grady nodded and slipped down the alley to the back door of the mine-supply store and went in.

Nita ran to him and hugged him tightly, then let him go and stepped back. "I was so worried that you were hurt. When I heard that rifle, I knew somebody had tried to shoot you again."

"We're about to close up, you want a home-cooked meal?" Adolph Gathers asked him.

"I'd love one, except I just ate with Orrin up at the Beanery. Now there is an interesting man."

Nita walked away to wait on a customer who was looking over the shovels.

"Nita told me more about yesterday. I won't ever

124

be able to repay you, O'Grady, for what you did for her," Gathers said.

"Sure you can, get her married off. After that kidnapping, I'd say she's more than ready for marriage."

"But she's only eighteen."

"I've known women who have three kids by the time they're eighteen."

"Me too, but don't tell Nita that."

"Tell her what?" Nita said, coming up to them.

"That I can't have supper with you tonight."

"Oh, damn!"

"Daughter! Watch your tongue. That's no way for a lady to talk."

"Well, I've got to be moving," O'Grady said. He waved and walked out of the store but could feel Nita's angry stare burning into his back.

15

Canyon O'Grady played a few games of poker at one of the better saloons, lost seven dollars, and then went back to his hotel, where he locked the door, wedged a chair under the knob so no one could break in without making a lot of noise, and then pushed the dresser in front of the window.

With his safety moves made, O'Grady went to bed and slept until six A.M. without waking. Today he had to earn his money. He would make a complete survey of the mines and see what the men thought of their hopes for a long-haul silver-mining operation. He hoped to peer into every hole, every shaft, and some of the drifts. All except the Bonanza. He wanted to talk to the men and get a good picture of the prospects for the hill. Then he had to write his report to President Buchanan.

He had breakfast at the hotel. The Beanery was closed this morning with a sign that said, "I'm rich. I quit. Good luck." It was signed Elly Handshoe. O'Grady grinned as he read it, and then walked up the slope to the first mine. It was a coyote hole in the ground that went straight down for ten feet. On the bottom two men with picks and shovels worked on the rocky soil scraping out enough to fill a five-gallon bucket, which was then cranked up on a rope that wound around a ten-inch-thick log.

When the bucket made it to the top, a third man grabbed it, carried it out twenty feet, and dumped it. The bucket was full of worthless rocks and dirt. Then the bucket went back down. While the bucket came up the rope, a second one on the bottom was filled by the two men. They unhooked the empty and hooked on the full one, and the man on top pulled it up.

"Been at this long?" O'Grady asked. He had been careful to wear trail pants and a blue shirt and no vest this morning. He had on an old hat that was soiled and sweat-streaked.

"No jobs here," one of the men answered. "Yeah, we been at it since sunup. The four of us own this claim and we're going to be rich, just like Elly and Sandy."

The next three holes he found were much the same. One was down over a hundred feet, with two tunnels off the shaft. The owners had not put square sets in them yet and had a cave-in, but nobody was hurt.

"Silver ore?" one of the men responded. "Sure, we're finding some, but just a shattered vein, like it got torn apart in an earthquake or something. We're looking for that solid vein twenty feet wide."

Aren't they all? O'Grady thought as he moved on. The next mine was one of the big producers, the King Mine. It had two shafts down a hundred feet and over a hundred feet of tunnels, each firmly supported with square sets to prevent cave-ins. In three places they had found small veins and were now following them toward what they hoped was the huge vein.

O'Grady went down to the first tunnel at the forty-foot level in a big bucket lowered by a capstan and cable and powered by a mule walking back and forth as the bucket descended or lifted.

O'Grady had been in a mine or two before and he

didn't like them. He went down now only to see for himself what the dig was like.

For a half-hour he talked with the mine head boss, a surly Irishman who had no use for a man without blisters on his hands. Then he saw the six-gun at O'Grady's side.

"And can you use the toy gun, laddie?" the man asked.

O'Grady grinned and dropped his hands to his side, then drew the weapon so quickly the big Irish miner jumped back a step. After that he told O'Grady what he wanted to know.

The foreman expected that the tunnel would follow the vein and that it would indeed hit a big vein. What they had was getting wider and better ore every day.

On top again, O'Grady watched the stacks of silver ore pile up. There was no good way to extract the silver from the ore yet in Virginia City. These first few months all of the rich ore was being taken down the mountain to a place it could be processed.

That system couldn't last. There would be too much ore here to move, and soon it would have to be put through a stamping mill to pound it into workable size.

That would come later.

He wandered the mountain all morning and then into the afternoon before he had what he needed: enough facts for his final report to President Buchanan. O'Grady went back to the hotel, wrote his report on the long-term chances of a real silver bonanza here, and sealed it in an envelope. He mailed it at the small post office. The letter would go out on the afternoon stage tomorrow.

There was a note in his box at the hotel when he went down for supper. "O'Grady, see me as soon as you can." It was signed Lila.

He went to the house of pleasure at once and asked

for Lila. She was busy. As he waited, a girl of no more than fourteen sat down beside him. She had almost no figure yet, nubs for breasts that showed through the thin, see-through robe. Her hips had not yet started to widen into womanhood and the muff of dark hair at her crotch was small and sparse. She didn't mind letting him see her.

"You like me?" she asked. "Some men really want a younger girl. Fresh and new. But I cost more. Ten dollars."

"Tanya, get back upstairs." The words came from Julia, who scowled at the young girl. "You're not supposed to be down here. And next time wear a proper robe."

Julia shook her head. "Yeah, she's young. But I got my start about her age. Here I have to have something for everyone. You're here to see Lila? Business or pleasure?"

"Business, Julia, strictly business."

"Lila is a nice girl. Don't hurt her, or you'll be looking at me and my sawed-off shotgun."

"No chance I'd hurt Lila."

A half-hour later Lila came into the parlor and they went for a quick walk outside along D Street. It was just turning dark.

"Punk was in to see me yesterday afternoon. Confirmed he was heading out of town and he'd be gone for a week or more. I told him to come back rich, and he said he aimed to. Then he asked me if I'd like to go to California and be with him. I wouldn't have to work anymore. He said he'd give me two thousand dollars that would be mine, I could do anything I wanted to do with it."

"Sounds like Punk is coming into some money. Payroll money maybe. He say if he was going with anyone from here?"

"No, he was riding out alone. Said he wanted something to remember me by for a week. Then he said he might not be back. He asked could I meet him in Carson City. I said maybe and he said he'd get in touch with me by letter. Now, all that sounds unusual."

"Like maybe he was going to hit the payroll and vanish down into California somewhere."

"Stealing from a thief. At least it's more of an honorable profession than just stealing."

They walked a moment without either speaking. Then she touched his arm. "Don't worry, I'm not going. I don't even like the man, let alone would I go off with him."

"Good. I knew you were a smart lady. You know anything about the payroll trip?"

"Nothing."

"That's quick. I'll see what the marshal knows. He should be notified about it coming into town." He reached out and took Lila's hand. "Thanks, Lila, thanks for helping. Telling me this is a good thing."

"Maybe it's about time I started doing something good, instead of just thinking about Lila."

"Might be, Lila. You'll never know for sure until you try. A lot of people out in this old world of ours could use a helping hand."

He reached out and kissed her soft cheek, turned, and walked quickly through a vacant lot toward C Street on the slope above.

Marshal Ben Jones was out checking door handles on the stores up and down C Street. O'Grady found him at the end of the street as he crossed over and came back toward the livery stable.

" 'Evening, Marshal," O'Grady said.

"Ah, the drifter from Washington, D.C. What are you up to tonight?"

"Looking for some information."

Five minutes later, O'Grady knew all the marshal did about the payroll runs. Yes, they notified him when the run would be made. It was coming up from Carson City's Utah bank on Friday. They usually left about nine in the morning. It was only eighteen miles, but mostly uphill.

"Usually takes about five hours, depending on the driver. They told me they were cutting down on the protection this time. You hear about some problem?"

O'Grady told him what he knew.

"Sounds like Punk Buolic is going to try to take down the stage and, from what you've said, light out for California."

"Where would be the best spot to hit the coach?" O'Grady asked the local man.

"On a steep upgrade where they slow to a walk. There's half a dozen places like that. This is Thursday night. You interested in taking a small ride and meeting that stage in the morning?"

"Figured I was going to ride shotgun about a quarter of a mile behind it. If anything happened, I'd ride up and discourage any wrongdoing."

"Damn, sounds like fun," Marshal Jones said. His eyes sparkled. "I got me a Henry I'm bringing. I can get you a Henry or a Spencer."

"Make it a Spencer and about six full tubes. That should be enough to discourage a few raiders."

"How many guns will Punk have, you figure?" the marshal asked.

"Four men in the stage with rifles. I'd say Punk would want at least four, maybe five or six. How much cash will be on the coach?"

"That I do know, it's on the report. Each mine is bringing in fourteen thousand dollars this time, that's fifty-six thousand all together."

"Worth taking a chance for, I'd guess. We better ride tonight and let our horses rest some before daylight. But first I want my supper."

They rode out of Virginia City about eight that evening. O'Grady had made it to the general store just before it closed and put three days' worth of food in his saddlebags. Both he and Jones had full canteens and their rifles in the saddle boots.

"Figure it will take us about four hours to make the ride, moving downhill most of the way," Marshal Jones said.

"We can get six hours of sleep and have breakfast before the stage comes past."

"What if we're wrong about the robbery, O'Grady?"

"Then we tail the stage by a quarter of a mile all the way back to Virginia City and nobody is the wiser or the poorer for our little ride." O'Grady snorted. "But that won't happen. I trust this lady, and I don't think she'd give us a wrong steer on this one."

The ride that night toward Carson City went smoothly and they stopped a mile outside of the little town near a small stream.

"Punk wouldn't try anything this close to town," Marshal Jones said. "He'll wait until the rig has to slow down for some of those uphill runs and the sharp cutbacks."

"By then the guards will be getting tired and bored as well," O'Grady said.

"They won't even leave until nine A.M. Time for some sleep."

They didn't make a fire, just had a long drink from the clear little stream and stretched out on their blankets and slept.

* * *

The next morning at six, O'Grady was up, making a small cooking fire. Smoke wouldn't matter here. He fried bacon and the smell roused the lawman, who lifted up on his elbows and couldn't believe his nose.

"You brought along food? I thought we'd go into town."

"No sense your being spotted down here," O'Grady said. "How many hotcakes do you want, five or six?"

They had bacon and hotcakes and even hot syrup O'Grady had brought along in a jar and heated. They finished eating, cleaned up, put out the fire, and it was still not seven o'clock. The sun was up warm and bright, and only a few clouds scattered the blue sky. It would be a fine day.

For half an hour they let the horses graze on the new grass along the creek, then they saddled them and loaded the saddlebags and made ready for the ride.

"They won't have any guards on horseback this time?" Marshal Jones asked.

"What the man said. Evidently the owners think they have the routine worked out so they can use fewer guards."

"Sounds like a good way to save a penny and lose fourteen thousand dollars," Marshal Jones said.

"We'll know that for certain before the day's over," Canyon O'Grady said, his mouth set in a firm, hard line.

16

Clint Nanson looked sixteen, but he claimed he was nineteen, and he had a paper that proved it. He was on his first payroll guard job and a little nervous. He snaked one hand back through blond hair to comb it out of his eyes.

"You say all we do is ride up the road to Virginia City and deliver one of these boxes to each of the mines, and that's it?"

John Lord grinned. "Not quite that easy if something goes wrong. Say about twenty Paiutes take it in their heads to get rich. Shoot this old tub full of burning arrows and scalp us or roast our heads over a slow-burning fire. They got all sorts of fun ways to kill a man."

"Paiutes ain't no worry," a third voice chimed in as the coach rolled out of Carson City. "We got to watch for them damn stagecoach robbers. Some hit down near Sacramento twice in one day last week. Sheriff said he figured they'd come up this way. Ain't no secret what we got in them boxes there."

The third man was Harry Wynant, an old-timer who was on his third ride as a payroll guard. He loved to tell wild stories and see the younger men cringe and get scared.

Between the four men in the coach on the center seat, tied down securely with wire, sat the four boxes of paper bills and gold pieces. The men didn't know how much was there but they figured about fifty thousand dollars.

They had been joking about what they could do with the money in San Francisco at one of the fancy gambling halls.

"Wouldn't last me but one night," Wynant said, pulling at his gray beard. "I'd hit the roulette wheel and plunge until it was all gone. Nobody ever wins in them places, but it sure would be fun while it lasted."

The four men settled down into their own private worlds for a while. Nobody talked. Some looked out the open sides of the rig, others checked the rifles and pistols each carried.

Two hours later they were getting restless. The day's trip was about half over and nothing had happened. They rode, watching out the windows, looking ahead, now and then looking behind them.

Nothing.

Good, some of them thought. They would be glad to get back to work at their regular guard jobs where you knew just about what was going to be happening each day.

Punk Buolic grinned when he heard the coach coming up the grade. He could tell it was moving at a walk. He was ready. He had recruited five men the day before and coached them carefully in what they would do. He had taken them into the hills and camped out last night to be sure none of them got drunk and vanished. This morning he had paid each man twenty dollars, with the assurance that they each would get thirty more dollars as soon as the job was done.

"Why we have to ride into California?" one of the men asked.

His friend hit him on the shoulder. "So nobody can

find us or identify us, stupid. You just do what I do and you'll be fine."

They were ready, eager for the next payment, not worried if they had to kill one or two of the guards to get the gold. With the horses was one pack animal, a horse with a pack rig made to carry a hundred pounds. The payroll wouldn't be that heavy. It was mostly paper money these days.

Punk had it figured out. They would shoot one horse to stop the rig, then all five of the men in and on the payroll coach would die. He'd pay off the five men he hired and make damn sure they rode off. Then he'd take the payroll, pack it on the horse, and ride for Sacramento. He had his own saddlebags packed with enough food for five or six days. He should make Sacramento in two or three. From there on he would get a boat to San Francisco and nobody would ever find him. Especially not Edwin Moudry of the Bonanza Mine.

Nobody would call him Punk again. He would be Charles Buolic. He'd always liked the name Charles.

The coach came closer. He could hear the breathing of the horses now as they tugged the coach up the slope. He checked his men. Three on the far side, two and him on this side. The first man was instructed to kill the lead horse, then get the driver. The other men were to fire into the coach as fast as they could, and at any targets that showed. It shouldn't take long. It all depended on the timing.

Punk saw the nose of the first horse coming around the bend in the switchback. He lifted his rifle . . .

Two hundred yards behind the payroll coach, Marshal Ben Jones urged his horse faster to close the gap on the rig.

"This could be it," he called. "Damn steep ahead."

Twice before they had closed in to about fifty yards of the coach as it vanished around sharp curves that the marshal knew were just in front of steep rises, but there had been no attack. Now they did it again. They were less than twenty-five yards from the sharp curve when they heard the first rifle shots. Both men had agreed that they would fire pistols the moment they heard any shooting ahead. It might be a surprise enough to throw off the attackers' aim.

They pulled pistols and fired three times each as they charged forward. There were more shots ahead, then the two horsemen raced around the corner. The coach had stopped about thirty yards ahead. Gunfire came from both sides of the road.

On the ride the two lawmen had worked out a strategy, now each rode into the brush along opposite sides of the road, dragging their rifles with them. The brush and trees here were minimal, and O'Grady leapt from Cormack and slapped him away to the rear. He dived behind a stump and looked uphill. Two men lay behind logs firing at the coach.

His first shot from the Spencer hit one rifleman in the chest and knocked him down the slope. The second one looked up and started to run, but O'Grady's next .52-caliber slug from the Spencer hit the man in the left shoulder, spun him around, and dropped him into the dirt.

Rifle fire from the other side of the road tapered off. O'Grady lay quietly watching the scant brush and few pine trees ahead of him. It paid off. A form lifted up and darted into some thicker brush, and a moment later O'Grady heard saddle leather creak as someone mounted.

This, too, had been talked about. If one or more of

the attackers ran, the lawmen would chase them and then come back for the survivors in the coach.

O'Grady whistled twice with his fingers between his teeth, and a moment later the big golden horse with the white mane came trotting toward him. O'Grady slapped Cormack on the side of the neck and leapt into the saddle and rode uphill. He charged through the brush then stopped and listened.

Far ahead he heard brush snapping and crashing. He and Cormack jolted in that direction. Soon he had a trail of the running horse through the dry pine country that was fast becoming little more than a sagebrush mountain.

The horseman must know the area. He reversed direction quickly, hitting a small watercourse with a few green trees and enough brush to cover him. He was riding hard, and O'Grady knew the horse would not last more than an hour at that rate. He settled in with Cormack, letting the big palomino trot along at his own pace as they moved down hill and into an island of green timber.

It was pine, which meant little undergrowth, and made it easier to see ahead. Twice he caught sight of the rider, a man in a gray hat and a blue shirt. There was no chance for a shot.

Twenty minutes later and more than a mile from the attack point, O'Grady came to a spot where the rider had gone into the small stream and hadn't come out. O'Grady splashed Cormack down the hock-deep water and looked on both sides of the stream.

The shot took Canyon by surprise, slashed into his left arm, and spun him half out of the saddle. Only the solid placement of his boots in the wide wooden stirrups held him in place. He bent over Cormack's neck, sliding half out of the saddle and away from the sound of the gunshot, and rode into some heavy brush to the left of the water.

O'Grady felt blood soaking his sleeve to his elbow and running down his left forearm. He had to get the blood stopped. Trying not to make a sound, he slid off the golden mount. Then he pulled out the Spencer and slapped the big gold on the flank.

It was part of a game they often played. He sent Cormack away, then whistled, and the palomino came back and tried to find O'Grady. The game had a purpose, and now the government agent hoped it worked. He ripped off his neckerchief and, holding one end in his mouth, wrapped the middle of it and the other end around his left arm where the slug had gone through. It bled a steady stream.

Now he could hold the short end in his mouth and wrap the longer end around, then tie it in a granny knot by holding one end in his mouth. He checked it. The blood flow had almost stopped.

He had been listening as he worked. Cormack had run maybe fifty yards downstream. At the same time he heard movement on the far side of the stream. The bastard probably rode downstream, came out, and doubled back for the ambush.

O'Grady hoped the bushwhacker had taken the bait and followed Cormack. Now he whistled through his teeth, then charged across the ankle-deep stream and hid behind a pair of pines on the far side.

If the man followed Cormack once, he might again. But the whistle would alert him where O'Grady really was. He might come back now knowing he was unhorsed.

Either way it was a chance to get the man in his sights. As he waited, O'Grady quickly reloaded two chambers on his six-gun, then lifted the Spencer to be ready.

A minute or so later he heard Cormack coming at a trot, not trying to be quiet, just covering the shortest distance between him and his master. The big golden stallion arrived where O'Grady had been and stopped.

Downstream, O'Grady heard movement, but could see no one. The shooter would still be on his horse. He might be waiting for O'Grady to go to the horse. Let him wait.

Cormack stood where he was as he had been trained. If he couldn't find O'Grady, he was supposed to wait at the last scent of the man.

Movement downstream. Some brush wavered, stopped, then moved again, and the head of a horse came through, then stopped. Canyon could chance a shot. But what if the rider was Marshal Jones? He had to wait. He could kill the horse, but then the rider would vanish on foot into the brush.

O'Grady judged the distance. Thirty yards to the horseman. He found an egg-size rock, discarded that for one twice the size, and lifted up and threw the rock in front of the horse. The rock crashed through the brush, hitting some dead branches, and made more sound than it ordinarily would.

The rider sent the horse bounding ahead three long strides. He was the man in the gray hat and blue shirt. O'Grady lifted the Spencer, which he had grabbed as soon as he threw the rock. He had little time to aim and the target was moving, but he fired. The round snarled through the rider's right arm and jolted him off the saddle to the ground. The horse trotted away and O'Grady rolled away from the blue pall of smoke from his shot and hid behind another tree.

He looked for movement where the rider had to have landed. Nothing. Again he used his patience and waited. At last he saw a tree branch move, followed by the slow movement of a blue shirt sleeve.

O'Grady put a Spencer .52-caliber round through the leaves directly in front of the figure.

"Move again and you're dead," O'Grady thundered.

The figure stopped.

"Stand up and walk forward into the open if you want to live more than about ten seconds."

The figure stood. He'd lost his hat. He held his right arm tightly with his left hand.

"For God's sakes, stop the bleeding or I'm dead anyway."

"What's your name?"

"Nobody you'd know."

"Your name or I shoot your right kneecap. You want to go on walking?"

"Christ, you'd do it. I'm Punk Buolic."

"Good. You work for Ed Moudry at the Bonanza Mine?"

"Yeah, yeah. Now tie up my arm."

"And he gave you orders to steal the payroll?"

"Yes, dammit. Now the bandage!"

O'Grady cut off the man's shirt sleeve, tore it into strips, and used the man's handkerchief to make a pad over the wound and tie up his right arm. It stopped the bleeding.

"How many men you use to bushwhack the coach?"

"Five and me, but you killed two of them already," Punk said.

"I should have made it three."

A half-hour later they rode up the trail to where the coach stood in the middle of the road. One of the horses was down and dead in the traces. Marshal Jones' horse stood tied to the back of the rig. To one side of the road he saw movement.

Jones came out grinning. "Figured you were having a ride in the country. I see you got him."

"Punk himself. What happened here?"

"The men inside the coach killed one of the attackers. I got another one, and the last one slipped away in the brush. We caught his horse, so he'll have a long walk. The driver is dead along with two of the guards."

"Two is better than four. Remember what we talked about if we stopped the robbery?"

Marshal Jones grinned. "Damn right. If we can make Punk testify, we've got two witnesses against Moudry on a murder charge with six bodies. But I still like your plan better."

"When were you supposed to bring back the money to Moudry, Punk?"

"Tomorrow, after dark." He looked at them. "What . . . what's going to happen to me?"

"You'll hang—you were the cause of six killings," Marshal Jones explained. "You'll hang sure as hell if you don't go along with our plan. You help us nail Moudry and we'll see that you only get twenty years in prison instead of hanging. Agreed?"

O'Grady scowled. "Hell, Marshal. I say we just run him down the road and have some target practice. We can say he was killed trying to escape."

Punk watched O'Grady with a long look. He turned back to the federal lawman.

"Marshal, I'll cooperate in every way I can. Do anything you want me to do to help convict Moudry. Just so I don't hang."

"You keep talking that way, Punk, and you may live to be an old man."

"Let's get this dead horse cut out of the traces," O'Grady said. "The three horses will have to pull the rig the rest of the way. We'll take the two dead guards and the driver back with us. The others will make a nice meal for the buzzards."

It was an hour before they got their little caravan rolling. They found the dead raider's horses and tied them behind the coach, including the packhorse.

Punk was put inside, tied hand and foot. One of the guards could drive a team and he took over the high seat.

Two miles below Virginia City they pulled the coach off the road along a tiny hint of water and into some trees.

"We'll stay here tonight and tomorrow," O'Grady said. "Then we'll have a little surprise for Mr. Moudry."

17

That evening around the campfire, they ate some of the food O'Grady had brought, and the agent told them what was going on.

"We could ride back into town and put Punk in jail and then try to convict Edwin Moudry of conspiracy and robbery and murder. We might win and we might not. This way we have a better chance."

"What we going to do?" Harry Wynant asked.

"All you men have to do is just sit tight and wait for us to come and get you. The marshal and I and Punk will be busy. Moudry expects Punk to come to his place tomorrow night with the payroll. So he'll go. Only Marshal Jones and I will be there as witnesses to listen carefully to what Moudry says to Punk."

"So we get to go home tomorrow night?" the other guard asked.

"Just as soon as we get Moudry on the hot seat. If either of you show up in town too soon, you'll tip our hand and Moudry will find out and know his plan went wrong. I want your word that you men will stay here tonight and tomorrow."

"Yeah, sure," Wynant said. "Be damn glad to see Moudry get his just reward. I don't like being set up to be killed. Especially by the guy I used to work for."

"Good. Now get some sleep. We'll talk about it

again tomorrow. We've got all day to lay around and rest up."

Marshal Jones checked both men's arm wounds and rebandaged them to make sure they weren't bleeding. "Looks like you'll both live," he said. Then he tied up Punk hand and foot. He fastened a rope from Punk's hands to one tree and another rope from his feet to another tree, leaving him just enough room to roll over. "Don't exactly want you going anywhere to-night, Punk. I'm a light sleeper. You even try to get away and I'll whack you with this big stick I've got here."

Punk seemed resigned to his fate. "I tried running once. All it got me was a shot-up arm. I ain't going nowhere."

The next morning Punk was still there. They found food in Punk's saddlebags and helped themselves to enough for breakfast and saved some for an early sup-per.

O'Grady saddled Cormack and said he would work on some training for the palomino. First he played hide-and-seek with the big golden stallion. Then he mounted and rode him directly for a tree. O'Grady had let the reins hang loose and at the last minute nudged the big animal with his right knee to turn him to the left.

Six times they did the same routine, then O'Grady gave the test. He rode the same way, with both hands holding his Spencer and aiming it ready to fire but without going for the tree. Then he nudged the stallion with his right knee and the horse turned to the left the same as he had before when the tree had been there. At once O'Grady scratched the big mount's ears to show his approval.

For two hours O'Grady worked with the palomino,

teaching him to respond to pressure by his knees and toes. He was satisfied when he came back and washed his face in the small stream they camped beside.

"Never seen that before," Marshal Jones said.

"Ever seen a Comanche or a Sioux warrior riding his war pony? These men are some of the finest riders I've ever seen. They learn how to ride when they are big enough to walk. By the time they are ten or eleven they have a young pony that will grow up with them to be their war pony.

"They spend four to six hours a day riding, attacking, shooting their bow off the back of the mount. They soon teach the war pony to move at the slightest touch of knee, thigh, or toe. The horse can be directed perfectly without the use of the reins.

"This leaves the warrior free to use both his hands for fighting, throwing a spear, firing a bow and arrow or a rifle. They get so good they can lean off either side of the horse, holding on by one foot under a sur-cingle, and lean down under the war pony's neck and fire their bow and arrow. They come riding at you and suddenly all you have to shoot at is one redskin foot, or the side of the horse."

"Damn, looks like you're coming close with Cormack to what the Indians can do," one of the guards said.

"Not even sniffing close yet," O'Grady said. "If I could work Cormack for three months, every day for two or three hours, I'd be making some headway. Now all I want to do is to be able to use both hands on my Spencer and still guide the horse."

The other two men admitted they weren't much at riding a horse. Both had been miners most of their lives. For an hour O'Grady and Marshal Jones questioned Punk Buolic about how and where he would deliver the payroll to the mine and what route he would take to get there.

Slowly the two lawmen worked out how they would do it and how they would work through the guards around the mine.

Then they took naps. "We're going to be up some of the night, so we better get some sleep now," O'Grady said. He named one of the guards to stand watch and he and the marshal lay down to try to sleep.

Just as darkness shadowed the mountain, the two lawmen loaded the money boxes back on the pack-horse and mounted up. O'Grady let Punk Buolic lead off. He had his six-gun in his holster and a rifle over his saddle, but both were without any rounds.

"Go in the same way you would have if you had decided to bring the money back. Don't attract any attention of the other mines or miners, or you're a dead man, understand?"

"Yeah, I know. You've told me three times already."

"It takes at least three times to get an idea through that thick skull of yours. Now move."

They rode up the small valley and cut over the ridge line so they would come up just south of town and before they rode near most of the mines and claims.

They went well to one side of the Ophir and around the Big Strike Mine. When the dark blobs of the Bonanza Mine loomed ahead of them, they stopped.

"Punk, you remember exactly what to do?" Marshal Jones asked.

"Right. I'm to ride in with the payroll, tell the guards I've got two men with me so you can get through. I leave you with the packhorse and I go in and see Moudry. My job is to bring Moudry down to see the money. I'll turn it over to him and get rid of the responsibility. I tell him that all of the guards and the driver were killed and the men who helped me are paid off and in California by now.''

"Then you ask him to be sure that's how he wanted it done," O'Grady said, breaking in. "Don't forget that part."

"Yeah. I know. Then I ask him for a hundred-dollar bonus for doing his killing for him. As soon as he admits that, the two of you will close in and take him into custody."

"What about guards around the mine?" O'Grady asked. "Are there any on horseback or just around the buildings?"

"Just around the buildings. I'll talk to them and tell them you're with me. No problem."

"Remember, Punk. We let you go so you can go upstairs and talk to Moudry. If you don't do that, we hunt you down and kill you, understand? This is about as rugged as it can get. You do what we say, or you're dead."

"Don't worry. I plan on living to be an old man."

They rode ahead and past one of the shaft openings, then toward the main building. About fifty yards away someone called out and they stopped.

"Who the hell's riding in here?" the voice asked.

"Punk Buolic, that's who, jackass. You want to keep your job, you lower that shotgun and get out of the way. I'm on a special job for Mr. Moudry."

In the short silence that followed, O'Grady drew his six-gun ready to cock it.

"Yeah, yeah, Punk. Thought you went down to Carson City."

"Where the hell you think I'm coming back from? Now get back on your post. These two guys are with me, and probably you're in their sights right now. Don't kill him, men."

"I agree, don't shoot. Still, damn unusual you riding in here this time of day."

"Worry about it." The three horses and the pack animal moved forward at a walk toward the office. They met no more guards and stopped at a back door. All dismounted.

"Remember your job, Punk—or be ready to die," O'Grady said. "Now go see him and get him down here."

The two lawmen waited in the shadows for five minutes.

"We shouldn't have trusted him," Marshal Jones said.

"Hell, we win either way. I think he'll be back. Moudry might have been in bed or poking that whore he bought. Don't panic yet."

Another two minutes and they heard someone coming. A man in front carried a lamp. The lamp-holder was Punk.

"Yes, sir, I want you to see it and turn it over to you. I don't want the responsibility. Must be fifty thousand dollars here."

"Damn well better be," Edwin Moudry growled.

"Went just like you said. We killed the lead horse and nailed the driver, then we shot the other four like you told us to. That was the way you wanted us to do it, right?"

"What's all this damn talk? You got the payroll. Yes, dammit. I said to kill them all if you had to. That don't matter now." He untied the ropes on the pack saddle and lifted off one of the heavy cardboard boxes. It was strapped shut. When he had the straps off it, he lifted the top and Punk held over the lamp.

"Yeah, green and gold, money. Damn that's beautiful. It was worth having to kill those men to get it.

Now let's unload the other three boxes. They are the profit on this little venture."

"Hold it right there, Moudry," Marshal Jones barked. "You're under arrest for murder and robbery and conspiracy. Don't move or you get shot."

"What? Who are you? Let me see you." Moudry reached for the lamp and held it higher, then he threw it forward and darted the other way. The glass lamp burst on the rocky ground, scattering burning coal oil over the area, singeing Marshal Jones' feet.

O'Grady had been standing nearest to the mine-owner. When he threw the lamp, O'Grady burst after him, running hard, almost grabbing him before he got into the building. But Moudry bolted inside and closed the door.

Locked.

O'Grady stepped back and ran at the door, kicking hard with his right boot at the section right beside the lock. It splintered free and the door burst open. The front door was open as well, and O'Grady raced through the office and out the door.

He saw the mine-owner running toward a shaft. A bucket was just lowering into shaft one, and Moudry pushed a man off and stepped on board. By the time O'Grady got to the winch and stopped the mule lowering it, the bucket had already passed the first tunnel at the forty-foot level.

"Bring the bucket back up," O'Grady shouted. He fired a shot in the air to get the man's attention. The bucket came up, the miners jumped off and let O'Grady have it to himself as he stepped into the steel ore bucket and held on to the steel cable to ride down.

At the forty-foot level a torch burned. Canyon stepped off into the tunnel. This was the only place that Moudry could have left the bucket.

At once a derringer snarled from down the tunnel and a small round whispered past O'Grady's face.

"No good, Moudry. We've got you. Six men died in that payroll holdup. You're as guilty of murder as the ones who pulled the triggers. You hired the men. You pay the price. Not sure if we can hang you six times, but it's a thought."

Ahead in the tunnel there were torches every fifty feet. They left pools of blackness between. O'Grady ran from light to light along the narrow steel rails that brought out the small cars loaded with ore or with useless rock and dirt.

There had been no drifts off to the side and no branching of the tunnel. Moudry was somewhere ahead. After two more torches, O'Grady found where the tunnel did branch. His first thought was to check for tracks, but he had no light.

O'Grady ran back to the last torch, pulled it from its holder, and hurried back to the branching tunnel. Fresh shoe prints, smaller than O'Grady's boots, showed. Yes, Moudry was a small man.

O'Grady ran with the torch now, holding it to one side. Twenty feet down the tunnel another shot was fired, this one jolting into the handle of the torch. It knocked the torch out of O'Grady's hand, but he picked it up.

"Nice shooting, Moudry, but that was your last round. Most derringers don't come with six. What are you going to do now?"

There was no reply.

"This is a worked-out tunnel, Moudry. You must know that. No more torches, only mine. I hear rattlesnakes like to ball up in unused tunnels. You ever hear that? Hundreds of them sometimes. They get mad if anybody steps on them."

"Bastard!" The angry word came from the darkness ahead.

"You want to come out and surrender to the U.S. marshal, Moudry? A good lawyer might get you off with thirty years. Hell, that's better than hanging or being chewed up by two or three hungry rattlesnakes."

O'Grady was at the point where half a dozen small drifts had been cut into the sides of the main tunnel. These exploratory tunnels were where the miners searched for the vein of silver. Most ran only fifteen or twenty feet into the mountain.

Now O'Grady had to check each one as he came to them. He made certain he could see into the drifts without Moudry getting past him in the main tunnel.

"Damn, Moudry, it gets scary down here in the dark, all alone, and with the thought your next dark step might be into the middle of a churning mass of crazy-mad rattlesnakes."

"Bastard!" The voice was closer this time.

O'Grady checked the last drift and then looked ahead into the blackness of the tunnel.

"Nothing to do now but to throw three or four shots down there and see if I can find any human flesh. You ready for that, Moudry? Not a hell of a lot of places to hide from hot lead down here."

"I'll never give up."

"Suit yourself, Moudry. You know your chances with a jury better than I do. But I'd bet it would be a whole lot better than with, say, a thousand rattlesnakes."

"Stop talking about snakes. I hate snakes."

"Good. Why not just walk forward then, and as soon as I see you, I can keep the snakes away with my torch."

"No. One of these tunnels on the forty level leads

to another dry tunnel that I can use to get out to shaft number two. Then you'll be the one crying for help.''

"Don't seem reasonable, Moudry. This one hasn't been used for some time. Dust an inch deep in here. Oh, that's right. It's dark up there and you can't see. Hell, I can run you down in a minute or two.''

O'Grady held the torch in his left hand and the cocked six-gun in his right as he suddenly sprinted forward.

"No! No,'' Moudry yelled. Then O'Grady heard a smashing as if a board had broken.

Moudry's scream of terror jolted through the tunnel like a fading train whistle. O'Grady ran ahead, slowed, and waved the torch in front of him. He came to it a few yards forward. A one-board barricade had protected the start of a new shaft that sank into darkness below.

A maddening scream of unspeakable terror exploded from far down the shaft, then a hissing and rattling that O'Grady remembered well.

He took a piece of the broken barricade and lit it with the torch. The screams came again and again, revealing the mortal fear and agony of a tormented soul.

When the board burned brightly, O'Grady dropped it into the new shaft.

The burning board fell for thirty feet, then hit bottom. At once it was struck at by a dozen slithering snakes. The end of the board burned fiercely for a moment where a pocket of pitch had collected, and in the bright light O'Grady could see the form of Moudry at the far side of the uncompleted shaft.

He sat with his back against the wall, hands slapping away striking rattlesnakes in front of him until the reptiles fastened their fangs into his hand and arm and both fell to his sides. Another snake struck higher and hooked its fangs into Moudry's cheek.

Moudry's watering eyes went wide in the sudden light, then rolled back in his head, he slumped forward and fell facedown into the mass of snakes that struck him again and again and again.

Slowly the fire on the board burned out, leaving Moudry's lifeless body in total darkness.

18

Canyon O'Grady didn't get up until almost noon. Marshal Jones pounded on his door until the agent stumbled to it and moved the chair and unlocked it.

"Rise and shine," Jones said. "If you put some pants on, I'll buy you dinner, since it's a quarter of twelve."

"You get him out?"

"Of course, that's my job. A pair of hay hooks for a grappling iron and some sticks to knock off the snakes, and we had him out of there in twenty minutes. He was not a pretty corpse."

"Not many of them are." O'Grady dressed and shaved, combed his red hair, settled the brown hat on, and walked down to the hotel dining room.

"I'd guess the rest of the payroll got delivered."

"True, last night. I also sent two men out to bring in the coach and the three horses, and the two guards."

"You got statements from the witnesses, and from Punk? Now I suppose you want one from me."

"True enough. I was figuring that your work here must be about done and I didn't want you slipping out of town before I got my official deposition."

"Won't. What's for breakfast?"

An hour later, the deposition had been finished and Canyon O'Grady sat in the parlor of Julia Cosette's fancy woman's house talking with Lila.

"Figured you'd be back, cowboy. You're not a man to let a half a chance get away from him, are you, now?"

"Not if there's even half a chance. You meant what you said the other night about thinking more about people other than Lila?"

"Oh, damn. I knew when I said it—"

"That it was the truth, and you knew it. What more could you ask for: a man who loves you, a man who has a fine reputation in his field and is one of the very best at his work, and a man who would lay down and die for you."

"You seem to know an awful lot about another man, cowboy. Unless of course you're talking about yourself." She looked up at him and smiled. That was a good sign.

"Now, how can I set this up?" O'Grady said, thinking out loud. "I could take both of you to supper. No, he doesn't like fancy eating places and the Beanery is closed.

"How about a picnic?" Lila suggested. "I'll get our cook to whip up some fried chicken and other good things. Think that would get his attention?"

"For a man doing his own cooking, that would get you his total undivided and enthusiastic attention." O'Grady leaned back on the sofa. "Lila, you know this man? You've talked with him from time to time?"

"He used to come every couple of weeks. We'd make love soft and gentle and then talk. The man is a talker. I guess I know more about him and his family than I know about mine."

"This picnic . . . It isn't just a nice thing to do for the blind man, is it, Lila?"

She frowned as she watched him. "No. I don't have to be nice to people I don't like. And I can like anybody I want to."

"I wouldn't want a big buildup for Orrin only to have him let down and hurt."

She looked out the window for a minute, then looked back at O'Grady.

"O'Grady, I'm tired of this. I'm looking for something better. That could mean running my own whorehouse somewhere. I don't want to do that. I think about Orrin. He's a fine man, a good man, and a black man. He could take me away from this, and I could be good for him. I could be his eyes where he needs me. I can drive a rig, hitch up a buggy. I can split wood and cook and wash clothes and even have babies.

"Look, O'Grady. I don't know where this is going, but I'm content to let it start." She stood up. "Takes two hours to fix a good picnic supper. You con Orrin into going for a buggy ride. There's a nice spot down by that little creek about a mile south on the Carson City road."

O'Grady talked to Orrin a half-hour later.

"A picnic? I haven't been on a picnic for ten years."

"Good! Then you're going on one at four o'clock today. Get your cutting and stitching caught up, because I'm having fried chicken and the whole works cooked up proper. No fancy eatery, just a bit of a stream and the shade of some trees." O'Grady stopped and let the silence lengthen. "Orrin, you can come, can't you?"

"Yes, it might be a nice break in my routine."

"Good. See you right here at four this afternoon."

The picnic started out as a success. O'Grady had picked up Lila first and the food. Then, with that safely stowed, they pulled up in front of the saddle shop, in the buggy and found Orrin waiting beside the door.

"You're late, O'Grady," Orrin said as Canyon walked up.

"Sorry. Glad I don't work for you, Orrin. Come on now, smile, we've got company for our picnic."

"Company? Who, the marshal?"

"Not at all." O'Grady helped Orrin across the boardwalk and to the buggy.

Orrin paused, sniffed gently, and grinned. "I'll be damned, my favorite lady in the whole world, Lila. Hello, pretty lady. I'm glad we're going to have a picnic."

O'Grady handed him into the buggy and then put the reins in Lila's hands.

"Orrin, I'm sorry, but I just found out that I have to have my report done for the late-afternoon stage. I won't be able to come along on the picnic, after all. You two just run along. Lila knows the spot."

"Hoodwinked and bamboozled," Orrin said. Then he grinned. "But I'm loving every minute of it." He turned to Lila. "That is, Lila, if you don't mind being seen with me out in public."

Lila laughed. "You crazy nice man, that's my line. I'll be proud to drive right down C Street with you any day of the week. Now, let's get moving before that fried chicken gets cold."

"You're the driver," Orrin said. He turned to where O'Grady had been standing. "You schemer, I'll see you in my shop before you go. You haven't told me yet how you took care of Moudry."

"Tomorrow, Orrin. I'll talk to you tomorrow."

O'Grady watched them drive down the street, saw a few heads turn, and then the buggy was rolling south for the picnic.

The next stop for O'Grady was Doc Paulson. The medic looked at the bandage, shook his head, and cut it off; then he examined the bullet wound. "Might have nicked the bone but not by much. I'm going to paint this wound with alcohol. Have you had that done before?"

"No, but I'd wager it hurts a mite?"

"That it does." He sloshed some colorless fluid from a bottle over the wound and O'Grady sucked in a quick breath.

"That's it" the medic said. "Not quite sure why it helps, but it stops infection from starting." He wrapped up the wound after putting on some salve, then tied off the bandage. "Good as new in a week or two."

O'Grady paid him a dollar and headed for Gathers' mining-goods store. He needed one last talk with the first man he'd met in Virginia City.

Gathers was making arrangements with the foreman of the Ophir to buy a hundred shovels at a reduced price. Gathers was grinning when the man left.

"A great day to be doing business," he said. "Hear they dug Moudry out of his own mine this morning deader than a rattler's tail."

"True. Damn tough way to die."

"He had it coming," Gathers said. "Now the whole mountain can settle down to mining the way it should be done. I hear the stockholders are sending in a new man to run the Bonanza. Hope he's a good mining man who can also get along with the hired help."

"Sounds reasonable."

Nita came up showing a big smile, her long blond hair swirling around her shoulders. "I understand you're a big hero," she said.

"Just doing my job," O'Grady said.

"I'm glad you came. Now Daddy won't get smashed into his grave by some hired killer from Moudry. Maybe we can even make a little money for a change." She watched O'Grady. "What are you going to do now, skip out of town?"

159

"In a day or two. Get all of the legalities cleaned up here. Right now I'm about ready to go have a nap. I didn't get all the sleep I needed last night."

"You hear about Elly Handshoe?" Gathers asked. "They hit another vein six feet from the first one. Looks like Elly is going to be the richest woman on the mountain."

"Sounds like she deserves it." O'Grady turned to Adolph. "Well, I wanted to stop by and let you know you shouldn't have any more trouble. Thanks for your help getting to know the lay of the mountain here."

The two men shook hands and he looked at Nita.

"I helped, I should get a kiss on the cheek," she pouted.

O'Grady laughed and kissed her cheek and she smiled. He went out the front door and back to the hotel.

He had just taken off his vest in his room when a knock sounded on the door.

"Yes?" he called.

The knock came again. O'Grady drew his six-gun and stepped silently to the door, pushed against the wall, and turned the knob. When he opened the door an inch and looked out, he saw a pretty blue eye staring back at him. He pulled the door open. "Nita."

"You were expecting the queen of England?" She slipped inside and closed the door, turned the key, and then put her arms around his neck. "There is no chance I'm letting you out of town without pleasuring you at least three or four more times. I figure that right now is a good time to start." She kissed him, looked up at him, and grinned. "You aren't going to give me a bad time, now, are you?"

"About how nice girls don't go around ripping off their clothes and jumping into bed, and how your father would not be happy at all, and how this could ruin your reputation in town and your chances of marrying a nice young man?''

"You did think about it."

O'Grady laughed and bent and kissed her breast through the soft fabric of her print dress.

"Now that's the idea, O'Grady."

He caught her under her knees and lifted her in his arms and carried her to the bed. Gently he laid her down and stretched out beside her. "Now, beautiful young lady, just what did you have in mind?''

"I'll show you."

She did.

It was nearly six that evening when Nita put her clothes on and went to the store. She swore that she would see him again that evening if he was in his room. He didn't promise but told her she could wait for him.

He had one last bit of business. When he stopped in front of the saddle shop, he saw the door open and three lamps burning inside. Orrin bent over his bench, working on the front rigging of a saddle.

"You going to work all night?" O'Grady asked him as he stepped inside and let the screen door bang shut.

"Might. Daylight don't mean much to me like it does to some folks.''

"True, Orrin. Like working in a mine. Night shift is no harder than the day shift.''

"Sit and rest yourself. Heard you did good work last night.''

"Some say."

"I say." Orrin pulled a waxed heavy thread tight and pushed the needle through the leather again with a pair of pliers.

"How was the fried chicken?"

Orrin turned, his black face beaming. "Damn glad you finally got around to the important part. Fried chicken was good. I ate a drumstick before we even got out of the buggy. Nice spot where we went. The food was great. Anything else you wondering about, meddling white man?''

O'Grady chuckled. ''Yeah, couple of things.''

''Might as well tell you, then. The biscuits were only fair. That satisfy you?''

Orrin lifted his head and grinned and they both laughed.

''Damn, O'Grady, I don't know what you said to that woman, but it must have been the right thing. She is so fine! Just so damned fine! I don't know how lucky a man can get. She moved out of Julia's place. We're staying back here in my digs. Lila says we don't have to move, but we both know we do. I've had an offer from Kansas. Some little town they say is gonna be the heartland of the cattle business. Waiting for a railroad. We'll be leaving here in a week.''

''Like to give you my hand on that, Orrin. Couldn't have happened to two nicer people.'' They shook hands.

''Still don't see what a beautiful girl like Lila wants with a dumb, blind fool like me. But she says she's happy. She also wants to see you a minute. Lila?''

She came through the curtain from the back of the shop. She wore a pretty pink blouse and her smile turned her attractive face into a work of beauty.

''Irish, thanks.'' She kissed his cheek. ''I don't know what to say.''

''Just take care of this man and be good to him.''

''No question about that. We'll always remember you.'' She touched his shoulder and he walked to the door.

''You two be good to each other, and write me a line now and then.''

Lila nodded.

Orrin waved. ''Get out of here, we got work to do.''

O'Grady let the screen door close softly as he left. Next he checked with the marshal. Everything was quiet. The territorial judge heard about the case and hurried into town. He set Punk Buolic's trial for next week and Punk already had a lawyer.

"I'll be here another day, then I'll be gone, Marshal. Anything else you need from me, let me know."

He shook hands with the marshal and headed back to the hotel. Supper. He hadn't had any supper yet. Maybe Nita would like some.

Another day here and then back to the wars. He wondered what assignment he would get next.

He was still considering it when he opened his hotel door. A lamp burned brightly. Nita Gathers sat on his bed wearing only her smile.

"I've been waiting for you," she said.

The government agent with the flame-red hair grinned as he closed the door, pushed a chair under the doorknob, and stepped toward the bed.

KEEP A LOOKOUT!

**The following is the opening section from the next novel in the action-packed new Signet Western series
CANYON O'GRADY**

CANYON O'GRADY #7

THE KING OF COLORADO

*June, 1860. Colorado—not a state, not yet a territory. All sorts of men with causes and schemes and dreams of wealth rushed into this virgin land hoping to ride a tornado to wealth and fortune. One of them wanted to become king, and did. . . .
The King of Colorado.*

A rifle shot slammed through the quiet Colorado mountain air, missing Shorty Balantine by six inches. He looked behind and saw five or six riders coming at him hard all with guns out. At once Shorty did what the government man had told him to do. He tied the reins, then jumped off the stagecoach and ran as far into the tall timber as he could get.

He panted as he looked back. Six masked riders had come up on the light celerity wagon, jerked the horses to a stop, and began tearing the rig apart. Shorty grinned when he saw the frustration on the men's faces. He edged closer so he could hear them, but still stay well out of sight.

"What the hell? Ain't no gold on this rig," one

masked man, the apparent leader said. "And no passengers. Spread out and try to find that little driver. I got some tough questions for him."

Shorty had figured as much. He squirmed deep down in the brush, pulling branches over him as he worked under a fallen pine tree. He had worn green and brown to make hiding easier.

The robbers hunted for him for half an hour, then gave up. The men then dropped their masks now that nobody could see them. The leader had a lean and mean face, hook nose, deep-set eyes, and wore a brown hat with a hole in the crown. His skin was leathery with a slightly yellow hue. His cheeks were shrunken and gaunt.

"Hell, we won't find him. Wid, you tie your mount to the back of this rig and get up there and drive. We can use it back in the valley for something."

They pulled out slowly as Shorty watched them go. When he was sure they were well down the road, he left the branches and walked to the rough wagon trail that led from Fort Collins to Denver across the top of the world.

Twenty-five yards back the way the coach had come, Shorty saw a man ride out of the brush on a stunning palomino stallion with a pure white tail and mane. He was the same man who had paid Shorty twenty dollars to drive the stage. The man rode up and nodded.

"Good job, Shorty. There's a bonus for you back in Fort Collins at the Colorado Saloon. Sorry you have to walk. I've got to keep up with this rig and find out where it's heading."

"Work for you anytime, O'Grady. Hope to see you again."

"Hope so myself," the man called O'Grady said. He rode down the wagon road following the light, high-built wagon that substituted as a stage coach for most companies on rough terrain routes.

Canyon O'Grady had to follow the rig but not let the highwaymen know he was there. Mostly he had to find out where they turned off. Since they took the rig with them, he figured they had to be working for the King of Colorado.

O'Grady rode tall in the saddle; his alert eyes saw every movement in the woods and kept a close watch on the tracks below him. His keen hearing let him ride just out of sight of the creaking celerity wagon ahead of him.

Canyon O'Grady wasn't sure what he would be riding into. This new assignment came directly from the president of the United States, and involved mail theft, kidnapping, and insurrection. That is, it did if he could believe all the reports he had read over the past few days.

Ahead the wagon had come to a stop on the main trail between Fort Collins and Denver. The area hadn't quite met all the qualifications yet to be a territory but the politicians said Colorado should conform within the next year.

The wagon sat there as O'Grady edged forward through the light timber just off the trail to determine what the stage robbers were doing. It was soon apparent. Two of the riders had tied ropes on the end of a two-foot-thick pine log along side the trail. Their horses strained to pull the small end of the log to one side.

As soon as the log was moved, the driver guided the rig past it and into a faint trail that led to the right. When the rig went into the trees past the log, the same two riders reversed their pull and dragged the log back into position. Then they brushed out the marks, brought in fresh leaf mold and small branches, and returned the area to what looked like a natural state. They wiped out the tracks of the celerity wagon with pine branches back twenty yards on the main road, then brushed out their own tracks as they headed into the brush back to their horses. The men mounted, making sure the side trail could not be noticed from the main trail, then rode forward to catch up with the wagon.

So that was why he hadn't been able to find any trails leading off to the right when he traveled this road twice the past few days, O'Grady decided. He touched his heels to the palomino and the horse move forward.

"Come on, Cormack lad, we have the scent now. We'll find this King of Colorado and turn him into a peasant."

O'Grady moved up closer now so he wouldn't lose the wagon. He kept back just enough so he could track them visually and watch for any kind of guards or lookouts along the trail as they passed.

The first one came less than three miles in from the main wagon road south. The wagon had rounded a small bend in the faint trail when the rig and its escort stopped, a log across the lane blocking it effectively.

Two of the men tied ropes to the log as before and used their horses to drag the pine log out of the way so the rig could pass.

"Wondered when you'd be back," a voice called from high on the slope to the left. O'Grady looked through trees, moved a little and then saw a man maybe a hundred feet up the side of a canyon waving with his rifle.

Guard number one. O'Grady figured there would be at least three along the way. Perhaps more at the other end of the trail if everything he had heard about the

King of Colorado was true. So far it looked much as the reports had told him.

The reports. There were always reports. This time he had been in Washington and the president asked to see him personally. Often his assignments came from some top level army staff officer with stars on his shoulder. This time President James Buchanan himself had ordered O'Grady front and center.

O'Grady had been inside the Executive Mansion several times by now, but it was always a thrill to walk up past the four great white pillars fronting the building and be allowed inside. An army officer always went with him as far as the president's private office door.

The big oval room was richly furnished with a plush carpet on the floor, and a huge cherrywood desk polished to a high sheen. A large, unfurled United States flag stood in one corner and the great seal of the president in the other one.

The president wore a stiff white collar over his white shirt fronted with a winged tie, a black frock coat, and afternoon trousers. President Buchanan stood and held out his hand as O'Grady was announced.

"Ah, yes, our Knight Errant. It's good to see you again, Canyon O'Grady."

"Thank you sir, it's good to be back."

The president motioned to a chair and O'Grady sat down. Buchanan watched his agent through his penetrating blue eyes. The president's pure white hair tufted sharply just above his forehead. That and his usual habit of cocking his head to one side was said by some to diminish his authority.

Canyon O'Grady had no such thoughts. The weight of President Buchanan's personality and the tremendous power of his office came through unfettered to O'Grady.

"What can I do for you, Mr. President?"

"You may remember that my father came from Ireland, just as yours did. So I'm thinking maybe we can double up on the luck of the Irish to get a small matter settled. Mr. O'Grady, have you ever heard of the King of Colorado?"

"The king. . . . No sir, I'm afraid not."

"Good, good. The fewer people who do hear of him the better. You'll get a complete report of everything we know about him. Briefly he was an ex-army Colonel with an exemplary record right up to the end. Then he went a little out of his mind and was retired.

"That was seven years ago. Now he turned up in the northeast section of Colorado where evidently he barricaded himself in some mountain valley and runs it like his own little kingdom. He even calls himself the King of Colorado."

"The army, sir?"

"As you know, our army is tied up right now with Indians and this other matter we may be facing shortly—secession. Fact is, we did send in a detachment, a fifteen-man scouting patrol with two officers. Only one man came back. He said he had played dead for two days before he could crawl away. The rest of the detail was slaughtered by superior numbers.

"Our main problem is the U.S. mail. We're proud of our ability to transport letters and mail across every state and territory in the union, and some not quite territories yet. This man's henchmen have attacked three stage coaches carrying U.S. mail, captured the coaches and all passengers, and neither the people nor the mail has been seen since."

"Yes sir, that is a problem."

"We have reports of other people missing in the area. The most recent event was another stage. The company sent armed guards along. Two of the three guards were gunned down, and the coach, the people, and the horses were all driven off somewhere and nothing has been heard of them.

"I want you to go out there, O'Grady, work your way into that damned 'Kingdom' find out what's going on and put a stop to it."

"Yes sir."

The president got up and walked to one of the windows and looked out on the lawn and trees. "I have reports that of our six U.S. Agents, you're the top man."

"I do my best, Mr. President," Canyon said smiling.

"They say you can think or fight your way out of the toughest situation. This might be one of those. I don't want to send in an army regiment. I'm looking to have this situation cleaned up and 'the king' dethroned as quickly as possible."

"I understand, Mr. President."

"Now, Mr. O'Grady. I can provide you with experts from the army: fighters, scouts, heliograph men, transportation, expense money, whatever you need."

"Sir, this sounds like something I need to work on alone. I'll have to infiltrate the area, scout it out, and figure how to dethrone this small king."

"Good. If you decide you'll need a company or two of infantry, you can come out and get the troops. We just can't send in men blind not knowing what they'll face."

"Agreed, sir. I'd expect you want this done as soon as possible, Mr. President?"

The fifteenth president of the United States nodded and O'Grady shook his hand and left. On his way out the army colonel who escorted him handed O'Grady a packet of material in a brown envelope.

"This matter is confidential, Mr. O'Grady. When you have read it and won't need it any more, your instructions are to burn it and stir the ashes. Understood?"

Now, staring at one of the King of Colorado's sentries who controlled the entryway through this small gorge, O'Grady had a better feel for his mission. The orders had been specific: to investigate and put an end to the King of Colorado. Sounded easy, but it was looking more complicated all the time.

O'Grady surveyed the possibilities: he could wait for darkness and slip through undetected. But he would lose the celerity wagon and miss finding other check points and lookouts.

He turned Cormack sharply to the left, working silently through the trees and up the gentle slope of the far side of the ravine. The sentry had been about one hundred feet up on a small ledge.

After five minutes of cautious movement, Cormack brought O'Grady to the right level on the slope. The cover gave way ahead, and O'Grady knew he would have to work on foot from there forward. He slid down from the big palomino, patted his neck, and tied him to a tree limb.

The U.S. agent moved with deliberate caution through the light brush and an occasional black oak. It took him ten minutes to walk and crawl through forty yards to a point where he could see the sentry.

The man had carved out a comfortable yet concealed lookout spot by cutting brush to cover the front of his small clearing, making a stool from cut branches and generally setting up a good little camp. He had a sleeping area there, a place for a small cooking fire, and a supply of food and provisions. He was a permanent lookout and might not be missed for three or four days.

The last ten yards were the slowest. O'Grady worked forward to a spot behind the white blossoms of a tall mountain mahogany bush, and peered around. The king's sentry was staring the other way at a redheaded woodpecker drilling a hole in a pinon pine tree's bark.

O'Grady lifted to his feet and silently walked the last ten feet, his six-inch bladed hunting knife out and ready. When O'Grady was four feet from the guard, the man must have sensed danger. He whirled, trying to draw his six-gun from his hip at the same time. The free-swinging holster flared outward, spoiling the man's grab, and by then O'Grady's knife lay against the sentry's throat. He now had the man's left hand twisted behind his back.

The guard swung his free right hand at the knife, hitting O'Grady's unprotected wrist. The movement powered O'Grady's arm downward, causing the blade to slice deeply through the guard's soft throat tissue and the left carotid artery. Blood suddenly surged outward, spurting six feet in the air.

The sentry tried to scream but could only gurgle. Blood came out. His eyes turned to see his killer and then went blank.

O'Grady dropped the dead man on the ground. With so much blood it would be impossible to fake a defection by the guard. O'Grady took some samples of the food supply, slid them into his small backpack and hurried over to Cormack. He had to catch up with the wagon in case there were more checkpoints.

LIFE ON THE FRONTIER

☐ **THE OCTOPUS by Frank Norris.** Rippling miles of grain in the San Joaquin Valley in California are the prize in a titanic struggle between the powerful farmers who grow the wheat and the railroad monopoly that controls its transportation. As the struggle flourishes it yields a grim harvest of death and disillusion, financial and moral ruin. "One of the few American novels to bring a significant episode from our history to life."—Robert Spiller   (524527—$4.95)

☐ **THE OUTCASTS OF POKER FLAT and Other Tales by Bret Harte.** Stories of 19th century Far West and the glorious fringe-inhabitants of Gold Rush California. Introduction by Wallace Stegner, Stanford University.
                                                                (523466—$4.50)

☐ **THE CALL OF THE WILD and Selected Stories by Jack London.** Foreword by Franklin Walker. The American author's vivid picture of the wild life of a dog and a man in the Alaska gold fields.   (523903—$2.50)

☐ **LAUGHING BOY by Oliver LaFarge.** The greatest novel yet written about the American Indian, this Pulitzer-prize winner has not been available in paperback for many years. It is, quite simply, the love story of Laughing Boy and Slim Girl—a beautifully written, poignant, moving account of an Indian marriage.   (522443—$3.50)

☐ **THE DEERSLAYER by James Fenimore Cooper.** The classic frontier saga of an idealistic youth, raised among the Indians, who emerges to face life with a nobility as pure and proud as the wilderness whose fierce beauty and freedom have claimed his heart.   (516451—$2.95)

☐ **THE OX-BOW INCIDENT by Walter Van Tilburg Clark.** A relentlessly honest novel of violence and quick justice in the Old West. Afterword by Walter Prescott Webb.   (523865—$3.95)

Prices slightly higher in Canada.

Buy them at your local

bookstore or use coupon

on next page for ordering.